Dead Aware:
A Zombie Journey

Eleanor Merry

CONTENTS

DEAD AWARE

ACKNOWLEDGMENTS

Thanks to my partner in crime, and in life, Fraser. Without your support (and help naming characters) I never could have finished this one.

My beautiful daughter Sayde. I finished, despite your best efforts at distraction. Nice try kid.

My family and friends who have supported me since day one and encouraged me to write this novel. You know who you are, and I love you for all you've done for me as a person and author.

To all of my beta readers, but particularly my mom who proved that family can be good critiques. Your input and support on this journey have been amazing. Love you mom!

Huge thanks to my cover artist, Brian Scutt, for not only creating me some beautiful covers, doing my formatting and images but also for his constant support. Your encouragement was invaluable, and I can't thank you enough.

To Sheila and Alex Shedd, my editors who helped elevate and polish my words.

My boss and friend, Corinne. You are such an amazing human being and mentor to me, I can't tell you how much that means to be able to enjoy your day job solely because your boss is great.

Also, in no particular order all of my amazing friends in the indie community that have been there to help me get to where I am today: Chris Miller, RJ Roles, Cassie Angler, Abby Akiyaw, David Simms, Nikki Noir, Scott Deegan, Aaron Bader, Holly Hill Mangin, Marissa Frosch, Robin Fuchs Brumfield and so so many more I honestly couldn't even list you all!.

It is not the monsters we should be afraid of; it is the people that don't recognize the same monsters inside of themselves.

Shannon L. Alder

PROLOGUE

Max had been in room 1201 at the Presidential Hotel in Toronto for the last few days since he died, and hadn't been able to figure out how to get out since. He woke up disoriented, with a ravenous hunger like nothing he could remember experiencing before. Truthfully, he couldn't recall much of anything before opening his eyes to the grey ceiling of the room.

Lifting his hands, he noticed a shiny band circling one of his fingers and knew this to be important but didn't know why. Vague impressions and ideas fluttered through his mind, but he couldn't make sense of them. The feeling of forgetfulness was strong and unnerving. He was sure he had been smarter, faster. It was like his memories and abilities were a word on the tip of his tongue that he knew, but just couldn't quite grasp or remember.

As he stood beside the window, he stared at the door with longing. He knew on the other side of it was freedom, but it was like his brain was processing things at a crawl, and he had yet to solve the riddle of the doorknob. On the first day he tried slamming his body against the door and, while it didn't exactly hurt, he somehow knew his body couldn't withstand that type of abuse. The word "pain" floated through his mind, but not the comprehension of what that meant. He tried the window, bashing it with uncoordinated fury. After a moment he noticed red seeping from his knuckles and put the tantalizing liquid to his mouth, humming lightly as he sucked it clean.

His stomach grumbled, and he howled along with it, unable to contain the building frustration inside of himself. He could smell something that called to him, stimulating his hunger. Something he couldn't quite put his finger on. Whiffs of *The Smell* kept pouring under the door and through the crack of the open window, permeating his senses completely, making him even more anxious and angry In the height of his anger, he tore apart the bedding in the room, ripping and clawing at the sheets until only ribbons remained. Feathers drifted through the air.

He walked over to the door again and banged on the doorknob a few times with his fists. He knew his escape had something to do with this and roared in anger when it still didn't move. Outside the room, something else roared with him.

CHAPTER 1

Clara mumbled curses to herself as she slammed the front door to her and Max's duplex home, which was unfortunately the only way to close it. The hinges were a bit off and the wood swelled over time, making that solid push the only way to shut it properly. There was also a several-inch gap at the bottom which allowed the cold in during the winter, and tended to be a convenient entrance for ants, and other pests, during the summer months.

Putting her keys and coat down, Clara groaned as she pulled off her shoes. She hadn't been leaving the house a lot lately, and her feet were unused to high heels. Walking down the narrow hallway into the kitchen she saw Max was busy doing something under the sink. Clara sat there for a moment, leaning against the counter and enjoying the view, which included a prime example of a cliché, the infamous plumber's crack.

Smirking, she shouted, "Hey baby, I'm home!", causing him to jump up and bash his head on the pipes above him.

"Ow, shi...Oh, hey." Max responded while rubbing his head. "You scared the crap outta me." Clara chuckled as she leaned over and planted a light kiss on top of his curly brown hair. Max smiled, looking up at his wife with adoration, before noticing the long shapely legs in front of him. This time it was his turn to smirk, causing Clara to give him a suspicious look.

"You know, sweetie, you are looking mighty fine this evening," Max said lightly as he ran his hand up her bare calf, "Dinner can wait a while, and I'm done here...." He trailed off and wagged his eyebrows at her suggestively, hoping the combined efforts of dinner, home repair and flattery would entice her in to their much-neglected bedroom. Clara smiled at him and moved her lips down to his. At this sign of acceptance, Max immediately grinned and pulled her down into his lap and began eagerly kissing her neck, making her giggle.

Sweeping her up, Max carried her to the bedroom, bridal style, and they didn't come out for quite some time.

———————————

Their home wasn't the nicest. They lived in a duplex in Surrey, just outside of Vancouver. It wasn't quite in the seedy area of town, but close enough to make it a lot more affordable. The block of homes had seen better days and the landlord who owned it was a negligent jerk. Despite this, or perhaps because of it, the occupants all bonded together and had ended up with their own happy little community. They all knew each other's names, which in today's day and age was unique. They had neighborhood barbecues in the summer and baby or pet-sat for each other when the occasion arose. All in all, it could have been a lot worse.

Max and Clara had been living there the last few years, and while Max was always slightly bitter he couldn't afford somewhere nicer for them, Clara didn't mind and was just glad they had a place to call home together. They had been friends since Clara was twelve and Max was thirteen. Later, he would brag that from the first time he saw her, he knew she was the one, and that he would marry her one day.

After Clara graduated high school, a year behind him, Max proposed and, of course, she said yes. Clara went to nursing school and Max completed a business degree. The rest, as they say, is history.

While they had their bad days, like any other couple, they were still in love after all these years and knew without a doubt that they would spend the rest of their days together.

———————————

After they finished in the bedroom, Max wandered back downstairs to finish dinner with a pleasant glow on his face. It wasn't until he remembered the news he had to tell Clara that his mood sank. In a few weeks he had to go on a work trip, and he didn't know how she would take it. He knew that for most couples, a few days apart wasn't a big deal, and was even considered a small break. But not for them.

They had been apart for less than a few weeks total over their almost twenty years together, and never for more than a few days. Over the last six months, Max had been avoiding this trip, not wanting to leave her alone. Unfortunately, his boss wasn't willing to push it any further. He would be heading out to Toronto in just over two weeks. A few years earlier, Max wouldn't have worried so much, though he still would have missed Clara. As of late, however, she had become incredibly withdrawn and depressed, and even getting her out of the house was a challenge. It was only recently that he had convinced her to start taking art classes, encouraging hobbies and more social activities within her comfort zone. Not that Max could blame her. Not after what happened.

They had been trying to get pregnant for years and were both overjoyed when finally, 6 months before, that little pee stick showed two lines. Max was ecstatic to be a father and spent hours talking, and singing, to Clara's flat belly.

By week 5, they had started choosing names.

By week 7, they had each picked up a few small items, a onesie here and there.

By week 9, the second bedroom had been cleared out to make room for a nursery, and they started telling friends and family.

But on week 12, Clara started bleeding.

In a panic, they rushed over to the hospital where Clara worked. Once they arrived the doctors checked Clara over and told the couple the words they were dreading; it was a miscarriage. She let out an ungodly howl upon hearing the word. A sound that would stay with Max forever. There was nothing to do but sit and wait for it to run its course. The sympathetic eyes of her colleagues burned into Clara's soul and Max would never forget the empty expression on her face that followed. They were sent home with some painkillers and the instruction for her to take it easy until it passed.

Max remembered that night vividly, despite his sincerest wishes to forget. The feeling of not being able to do anything to help his wife, or save his unborn child, was the worst thing he had ever experienced. He looked back often to try to come up with ways he could have changed things, saved their family. He came up short every time. More than their crappy house or anything else in their past, this was his worst regret, and their darkest moment.

They found out not long after that night that the heavy periods she had been experiencing the past few years were likely more miscarriages that had occurred very early. After that night, without asking, Max had picked up condoms and started using them.

Clara became depressed after this and stopped going into work. It was almost as bad, if not worse in some ways, having to go back and tell everyone they had already told about the pregnancy. Reliving the nightmare again and again. While the hospital she worked for understood, they also couldn't have a nurse who didn't show up for work, and she soon lost her job.

While Max did what he could to bring her out of her dark headspace, he still had to work to support them, but found that when he spent his days at the office he would often come home to Clara sitting alone, staring off into space. Compared to the happy and optimistic woman he married, it was a contrast that worried him.

They got by fine with his income, even if it was a bit tight, but Max knew that it was depression which prevented her from going back into nursing and not job availability like she claimed. He tried not to stress her out or put too much pressure on her to return to work. He was able to encourage her in other ways, like the weekly painting class, which seemed to be slowly rebuilding her confidence. He figured she would return to the workforce when she was ready. *One step at a time*, he would tell himself. *She's getting out of the house again; that's a good start.*

All of this went through Max's head, reliving it just like he had a thousand times before, as he stood and stirred the spaghetti. *At least tonight we actually had sex*, he reminded himself. She was as happy as he had seen her in a long time, and to keep her in good spirits he would spend some extra time with her in the coming weeks until he had to go.

He really did worry about leaving her alone, not wanting her to backtrack on the progress she had made, but he had been preparing this proposal for months and had no choice. Before he told her, he would finish the spaghetti—her favorite meal—and rub her feet. She could never resist a good foot rub.

After eating, and spoiling her, he would tell her.

While Max finished dinner, Clara bathed and thought about how lucky she was and how loved she felt. The problem with this, however, was that she also felt a selfish guilt for all the care he showered her with, especially lately.

Max had always been a loving and attentive partner, but ever since that night six months ago he had been even more so. In fact, since then, he was almost *too* doting. He treated her like she was breakable, afraid to cause any tension within their relationship.

At first, she had appreciated it, but it was slowly starting to grate on her. She wanted Max to feel like he could be himself with her and say what he wanted. Not that any couple wants to have strife or problems, but the complete lack of it for the last few months was starting to tempt her into picking small fights. She noticed herself doing it, saying or doing things she knew he didn't like just to try to provoke a reaction out of him. However, Max continued being the overprotective, non-confrontational version of himself despite whatever Clara did. She wondered if maybe they should look into couple's therapy or something but felt silly suggesting it. What would she say, anyway?

At the end of the day, Clara felt incredibly fortunate to have a partner who loved her as much as Max did. After she lost her job and she no longer contributed any income, the guilt became worse. On her darkest days, she had considered ways to free Max from herself. She would almost convince herself that suicide, or running away, was best for him. It was always right then that he would walk through the door at the end of his work day. He would smile at her and make her feel loved, and the guilt, while still present, would fade away, at least for a while. Even today getting back from her art class, he had come home, started dinner and was trying to fix the tiny leak she had noticed a few days before. Max truly just wanted to make her life better. For the moment, she willed herself to be grateful and happy for that.

She wrapped a robe around herself and looked in the mirror. Her blonde hair flowed behind her in a way she knew Max liked, and her skin glowed from the warmth of the shower. Smiling to herself, she put on a small spritz of his favorite perfume and went downstairs for dinner.

"So how long will you be gone for?" Clara asked, the slightest quiver in her voice betraying her true feelings at the idea.

Sensing the need for reassurance behind her question, Max stood up and enveloped her in a hug. Clara gave a small smile, understanding the gesture for what it was, and hugged him back tightly.

"Just a few days, baby. A week at most," he replied into her hair, not willing to let go of the warm hug yet. Despite how long they had been together, he could never get enough of this woman.

Pulling back to look at her, he noticed a stray tear and wiped it away. "Have I told you how proud I am of you lately, or how much I love you, my beautiful, sweet, loving wife?" Max sucked up, with a silly grin on his face. Clara giggled at his endearment. She was glad for the distraction. Smiling at his success, Max took her hand and brought her over to the couch, seating her comfortably in his lap.

"Have I told you how much I love you lately, my silly, sweet husband?" She replied jokingly, making Max chuckle and pull her closer.

"Nope, but I'll never tire of hearing it," Max replied cockily. "Now, enough of this nonsense. Why don't you tell me about what you did in your class today?"

The next day was Saturday, which Max knew was Clara's favorite day because it meant he wouldn't be working, and they could spend time together.

While during the week Max was up and out early, he tried to make a point of giving her something nice to wake up to on the weekends.

It was about 9am when Max crept upstairs with a huge spread of breakfast foods, including some hot, fresh coffee. Setting the tray aside, he crawled into the bed behind Clara and wrapped her in a big spoon. "Mmmm," she groaned, making Max chuckle lightly. She had never been a morning person and even less so since the miscarriage. *Oh well*, he thought. *You gotta kill it with kindness.*

He started planting light kisses over her shoulder, neck, and head as he hummed one of her favorite songs lightly. "Good morning sunshine," he whispered in her ear after a few minutes of his ministrations. "I brought coffee."

At this last part she turned around to look at him, giving him a small, sleepy smile. "Thanks, Max." Max smiled back at her, giving her one final kiss on her forehead before enthusiastically hopping out of bed and grabbing their breakfast.

While Clara got dressed, Max went back downstairs to inspect the sink he had been working on the day before. It drove Max nuts that their house was so old and run down. While he did his best to keep things in good repair, he often felt guilty for not providing a better place for them to live.

Cursing at the persistent drip, he made a mental note of the manufacturer and part he needed and went to see if Clara was up for a trip to the hardware store. His plans for the day included fixing the drip and doting on his wife. The sun was shining, and Max just knew it was going to be a good day.

CHAPTER 2

4 Weeks Later

World News:
An encephalitis virus, believed to have originated in Delhi, India, has now been reported in numerous cities across Europe. This flu-like virus is highly contagious, and those who experience symptoms are advised to see their health care provider immediately. More updates as they arise.

World News:
 FIRE (Fever Induced Rapid Encephalitis) is the name on everyone's lips regarding the recent epidemic sweeping across the globe. Several countries have enacted curfews in addition to other preventative measures to avoid the spread of the infection. While there are no reports outside of continental Europe and Asia, the highly contagious nature of this virus makes it likely that it will surface on other continents soon.
While we are still unsure of the fatality level of this virus, the rate of infection and high fever caused by the virus have made health care professionals around the globe concerned. W.H.O., the World Health Organization, are currently studying the virus and will provide updates as they know more.

ATTENTION CITIZENS OF CANADA:
The encephalitic virus dubbed FIRE has been sweeping its way across the globe. Initial reports came from Delhi, India, but about a week ago the first report in North America occurred in New York. Thunder Bay, Ontario was affected only a day later. At this time, W.H.O. is working around the clock to determine more of this virus's origins and possible effects. However, in the interim, they have advised that all citizens remain indoors wherever possible and stay away from anyone who is exhibiting signs of illness. We will

provide updates when we have more information on how it is spread. However, please be aware of the following symptoms: fever, lethargy, vomiting, diarrhea, photophobia, confusion, aggression, and seizures.

CANADA EMERGENCY BROADCAST UPDATE:

Reports of death caused by the FIRE virus have been coming in since yesterday. As we all know, it is highly contagious and seems to be airborne. Reports indicate that about 75% of those infected with the virus are dying within seven days of contraction, generally due to viral encephalitis. If anyone around you is showing a decline, it is strongly recommended that you remove yourselves from the vicinity immediately. Reports of those dying from the virus and getting up again have been coming in. While we have not verified anything at this time, we encourage citizens to remain vigilant.

The transmission cut off, and after that, the broadcasts ceased as communication systems went down over most of North America.

Max opened his eyes to a muted and slightly stained hotel room ceiling. He stared upwards for several minutes, still not mentally aware, even though he was awake physically. Finally blinking, he turned his head slightly, taking in the cheap hotel room around him.

Beige walls surrounded him, accented by the grime and filth underneath which covered both himself and the bed he laid on. Lifting his head slightly, Max took in the reds, pinks, and other vivid colours surrounding him. For a moment, the brightness mesmerized him as his brain processed the spectrum. He blinked again and frowned, looking upwards.

His head felt foggy and unsure, and he couldn't recall who he was, much less anything else. Straining his mind, he tried to recall where he was or why he was there, but he quickly came up short.

Unsure of what to do, Max tried to turn his body to pull himself off the bed, but overestimated his readiness. With a heavy thump, he tumbled off, not hurt but surprised by the suddenness with which he hit the floor. He shook himself off and pushed up off his hands.

Unsatisfied with his reaction time, but not quite comprehending what he was expecting, he finally managed to pull himself up to a sitting position back on the bed. Taking a moment to take stock, he looked down at his body and arms as he flexed his hands. *Before waking up, what was different?*

Inch by inch, he moved his whole body, analyzing his own movements and responses, before finally daring to stand again. Grinning as he was successful, he shambled around the room aimlessly, getting used to his clumsy legs.

An hour later, after wandering the room, Max came to recognize the door. He stood several feet away, head cocked, as he stared.

Door.

The word vaguely floated through his mind as he stared, concentrating hard.

Out.

He continued staring until he was pulled from his reverie by noises outside. Curious, he shambled over to the window to see what he was hearing.

The window was already open a few inches. However, Max couldn't seem to figure out how to make it open further. Pressing his nose to the glass and his ear to the open crack, he listened and watched.

Down below on the streets, he could see two groups of people. One of the groups seemed frantic, hiding behind big metal objects and shouting. The other group seemed to have a similar detriment to Max as they slowly approached the opposing group.

Max listened intently to the sounds drifting through the opening, trying to make sense of the noises coming from the one group. The idea that he should be able to understand them was a strong feeling. However, he quickly became more frustrated as he found himself unable to comprehend the words.

A few gunshots went off as the noisy group ran the other way, their voices fading into the distance while the shamblers trudged along behind them.

As Max watched them leave, he contemplated the vague triggers the voices had caused within his mind. Frustration filled him again and he shouted and banged his hand against the window.

By day two, his hunger had reached new heights. Earlier, he found some partially rotten food under a tray, which he had quickly devoured. He then started to look in the small attached room for more food. Finding a source of water, he drank his fill and was satiated for the moment. When he turned around, he saw something that surprised him. It was someone staring back at him in the mirror.

Max grunted a bit, walking up to it with his hand forward, reaching out to touch the person he was seeing. He knew it was himself really, but somehow his mind couldn't accept that logic.

He saw curly brown hair which was greasy and sticking out in all different directions. What really stood out was his skin, alabaster and devoid of colour other than brown fuzz covering his cheeks. There were a few thick veins that stood out against the paleness of his skin, and his lips were only slightly darker with a bit of a blue tinge.

And vivid blue eyes that stared straight back at him.

It wasn't what he expected to see. As he stared at himself, he wasn't sure what else he should have expected. He just knew it was wrong, different.

After that, he didn't look in that part of the room again and took to spending most of his time standing by the window, alternating between watching outside and looking at the door. After days of this passed, he heard more noises, but this time coming from the other side of the door. His stomach growled as he made his way across the room.

CHAPTER 3

In the days leading up to her death, Clara thought a lot about Max. She thought about what she would give to go back and beg him to stay. Would it have made a difference, she wondered, or would she still have died, just together?

The phones and the internet had been down for a few days now, so she had no way of contacting Max or knowing if he was okay. Electricity flickered in and out since the emergency broadcasts started. Clara had first secured the house and did what she could to prepare for what the news was calling the FIRE Virus. The first time Clara heard that name she shuddered, her inner nurse horrified at an illness that sounded so morbid and all-consuming.

Clara called Max at his hotel in a panic when she first heard the news. He had already been gone for two days and wasn't scheduled to come home for another five. "When will you get home?" she sniffled into the phone.

Max sighed, "It'll be okay, sweetie. It'll just be a few days until the government gets a handle on this thing. I'll see about renting a car and driving home if I have to. One way or another, I will come home to you, Clara. I promise."

The first reports were of illness outside of Delhi. Images of full hospitals and sick people filled every station. This was quickly followed by most of Europe, and the spread continued quickly. For a different reason now, it was a relief that she didn't have any work to go to, and she ended up watching a lot of news. It was terrifying and depressing and she understood that for any illness to spread so fast was incredibly unusual—and extremely dangerous. When she spoke with Max on the phone, he told her not to leave the house, he would be home within a few days, and everything would be fine.

It was then that the government stepped in and decided to put a halt to commercial air travel to prevent the spread of the disease. Even with so much news coverage, it seemed they knew little about the virus or how it started.

The attempts being made spoke of desperation. The only thing they did seem certain of was that it was highly contagious, and quite likely airborne. No one wanted the virus going further. Multiple governments, working with the World Healthcare Organization, were taking extreme measures to prevent further spread. Of course, they were too late, and it hit New York only a few days later.

It wasn't long after that mobile networks went down, constantly showing nothing but a 'Not In Service' message. Clara's landline had a dial tone, but nothing connected, no matter which phone number she tried. She wondered if the flickering electricity would be gone soon as well.

She got very lonely, and despite her misgivings, she had gone out a few times to check on the neighbors and find out what was happening.

A few people in their neighborhood had left before the news reports and broadcasts started getting more serious. Families planned to go to their cabins and other getaways to escape from cities, people, contagion. The streets were quiet, and it felt like the entire city was taking a deep breath. The calm before the storm.

There were several people that had stayed behind for various reasons, including their neighbor, Diana Waverly, who was an older woman that lived alone on the other side of their duplex. Her husband had died years before they had moved in, and Clara often went over and sat with her and kept her company over tea. It was comforting to them both to have someone to talk to. Diana reminded Clara of her own mother, who had passed away almost a decade ago now.

After the miscarriage, Clara had stopped going to visit. But once the virus hit she worried about how the older woman was doing and went over, despite Max's instruction to stay in, to make sure her neighbor was okay.

Shortly after arriving at Diana's, Clara realized how little food and water the woman had and knew her own pantry was not much better. Not heeding the warning bells ringing in her head, she went out to the store for both of them and was not a little terrified at how chaotic it was. The people who were out seemed frantic and fearful and no one spoke to one another. A miasma of hopelessness hung over the area sucking all good thoughts and feelings out of the air like a vacuum.

She hurriedly grabbed some pasta, canned foods and water and rushed back home as quickly as she could.

Diana, despite being a homebody, had gotten sick only the day after Clara had returned with supplies. While Clara did what she could for her friend, she couldn't do anything for the burning fever or seizures that plagued her. She considering leaving the city and heading out to a friend's farm for antibiotics; she knew they kept a large supply for their livestock. Before Diana progressed any further, she took a bottle of pills one night after Clara went home and fell asleep painlessly. Clara found her the next morning.

With no alternative, Clara placed a blanket over the Diana's body and left the apartment.

By that evening, she too had started coughing.

What started as a runny nose and cough quickly developed into a burning fever with vomiting and diarrhea. Her eyes seared in her skull, and she screamed in pain as the sensation shot down her neck and spine. For the first few days, she did her best to take care of herself, but by day five she was wavering in and out of consciousness. At first, she was disgusted with the state of the bed and herself, which were now covered in feces, urine and vomit. By the end, she was beyond caring. Even if she had cared, she wasn't capable of doing anything about it.

As she lay in bed in those final days, unable to even get herself a glass of water, Clara thought of her time with Max and all the memories they had made. More than anything she wished he was there, holding her. Clara knew if she was going to die, all she wanted was to be with him. He had promised to come home, but he hadn't. She didn't even know if he was still alive or not. Now she would die alone, in their bed, with nothing but her memories and a spoiled blanket. And the pictures.

When she had still been able to move, she had gotten some of their photo albums. She found herself grateful for the love of scrapbooking she had inherited from her mother, otherwise their memories would be lost along with the technology age. Photos were spread out around her, reminders of so many beautiful days. The first time they met, their first vacation, Max proposing, their Vegas wedding, their first ultrasound….

At the end, most of the pictures were ruined, covered in various disgusting bodily fluids. They crumpled under her body as it shuddered in its final throes. One picture she had held on to through it all—a simple photo of her and Max smiling, at the front door of their first house. She gasped for breath and heat burned behind her eyes as Clara held the photo to her chest and took her last breath.

Waking up had been a strange sensation for Clara. Her first impression had been one of hunger, followed very shortly by confusion. Of loss. Whether it was something, or someone, that she lost, she didn't know. She just knew she was hungry, lonely, and didn't know what had happened. Opening her eyes, she looked around and tried to remember who she was or where she was. Or what she was. She could smell the filthy sheets beneath her, but in this state, it didn't register as a bad smell. Just a smell.

She sat up and looked around, realizing she was holding something in her hand. She looked down at the picture, and while she couldn't quite remember why, she knew it was important for some reason. Clara slipped the picture into her robe pocket and moaned slightly as she got up to go in search of something to eat.

Her stomach moaned along with her.

CHAPTER 4

Max stared at the door with interest as he listened to the sounds on the other side, which seemed to be getting closer. After being inside this room for a few days he was very curious about anything new, especially noises. A few times he had heard different sounds in the distance, either from the window or distantly through the walls, but this was different. Grunting, he put his ear against the door to hear better.

Suddenly, the door swung open, pushing Max down as a quick, small body crashed into his. The heavy door slammed shut behind them and fists began pounding on it almost immediately. Max looked up and saw a youth of maybe thirteen staring at him, complete and abject horror in his eyes. Suddenly, Max smelled the tantalizing scent that had been drifting under the doors. In that moment, he realized it was coming from the boy.

Food?

He growled as the boy scrambled off him, backing into the corner. As Max willed his worthless body to get up, the boy saw his opportunity and ran past him into the bathroom. He slammed the door before Max could get to him. A lock clicked as Max reached the door. He banged on it a few times, mostly to compare it to the other door that had so far stymied him. While this door seemed lighter, he somehow knew he wouldn't have any more success with brute force on this one. He snarled in anger and smacked his hand against it one more time before walking back to the other door that he had wanted to get out of in the first place.

He could still hear shouts on the other side, and Max absently wondered who the boy had been running from. He listened for a quite a while before the sounds faded, although he was careful to not stay too close to the door this time in case someone else came in.

As soon as the room quieted, small sniffles could be heard coming from the bathroom. Max tried thumping on the door one more time and was rewarded with a small scream from the other side. Frowning, he tried it again, but this time he was greeted with silence.

A few hours later, Max was resting on the bed when he heard quiet whispers coming from the bathroom. This time, he recognized it for what it was.

Speech.

Words.

Comprehension?

He walked back over to the bathroom and listened.

"Our Father in heaven, hallowed be your name. Your kingdom come, your will be done, on earth as it is in heaven,"

Listening to the boy pray, Max felt an emotion that, while strangely familiar, was foreign in his current state. He still felt hunger, but The Smell from under the door seemed to have diminished, and with it his heightened sense of anxiety and anger. His brain started to make connections it hadn't before, and he pressed his ear against the door, eager to trigger more.

"And lead us not into temptation but deliver us from evil. Amen."

Max heard a loud sigh.

"Please, God, just…Fucking help me in here."

Max felt the urge to respond to the boy and opened his mouth to say something, but only a small moan escaped. He frowned. *I should be able to do this*, he thought. *I used to be able to do this.*

Determined, he thought for a moment, and his brain rewarded him with a word. Opening his mouth once more he tried a greeting,

"Haaihfgghthgfft."

Silence on the other side of the door.

It felt like his mind knew what he wanted to say, but his mouth just wouldn't cooperate. Frustrated, he tried again.

"Yahufsahhii."

The boy in the bathroom put his ear up against the door. As unbelievable as it seemed to him, he felt like the creature on the other side was trying to talk.

Before ending up at the hotel, the boy had been on the run for almost a week since his parents died. He had left almost immediately, and it didn't take him long to realize his parents likely were not dead any longer. At least, not in the traditional sense.

He had been very careful and had managed to mostly avoid run-ins with what he was pretty sure were zombies. With avoiding them also came a lot of hiding. That meant he had managed to observe their behavior quite a bit. While he had seen some of them do surprising things (at least compared to the comic books he used to read and shows he used to watch, where the undead were always just slow and stupid), he had yet to hear one talk. He wondered, if he went back home, would his parents would try to talk to him too?

Tentatively, the boy responded, "Hello?"

Max grunted in happiness at having received a response and gave the door a gentle knock.

"Are you trying to speak?"

As Max listened to the words, he could feel his brain connecting more pathways and memories forgotten with his death. That feeling of forgetting came back to him, but this time it wasn't accompanied with the feeling of hopelessness. He genuinely felt like he could remember.

"Huhhai," he let out finally, grinning at his quasi-success.

The boy became silent once more. He was right, wasn't he? The creature on the other side of the door just said hi to him!

"Can you understand me?" The boy asked through the door.

Max sat silently for a moment, digesting the words.

Suddenly it hit him like a train at full speed.

Words!

Holy shit!

"Yes!" Max replied excitedly. "I...understand." Max frowned for a moment at hearing his voice. Just like his appearance, his voice felt off somehow, but he didn't quite know in what way. Nevertheless, the pride from remembering words was strong.

The boy stared at the door in shock. *The zombie just spoke to me!*

After not hearing another voice for the last week, the relief of it washed over the boy. He stood up to walk over to the door and caught sight of himself in the mirror. What he saw worried him. His skin was devoid of colour with a faint blue tinge around his lips, his eyes bloodshot and red. It reminded him of his parents before they died. He looked down at the bite mark on his arm and turned on the tap to wash it once more, grateful the water was still running here. The places he had been to so far seem to vary with water and electricity. Not sure how to address the zombie further, he decided to start simple: "So...what's up?"

CHAPTER 5

Clara wandered the once familiar house in a daze. Walking down the stairs, she lightly touched the pictures on the walls, noting how most of them contained the same face of the man she held in her pocket. While it frustrated her to not know who he was, his image comforted her. She stopped at the bottom of the stairs, cooing slightly as she ran her finger down the man's face, smiling to herself. While she couldn't remember much, she knew this man was important somehow. Made her happy. She touched the picture in her pocket as she continued through the house. Her fuzzy robe trailed behind her.

As she wandered the place, Clara felt like she recognized many things, but her mind was foggy and unsure. Vague impressions fluttered through her brain but no single idea seemed to take hold. It was a frustrating feeling, made worse by her inability to follow through on any one thought process.

She passed by a particular room only to turn around and take a second look. Although the room was empty and appeared unfinished, it stirred vague memories within her. Small yellow animal patterns lined the wall. She stood a moment longer staring before the memory was overwhelmed by a rumbling in her stomach. Sniffing to find the source, she moved out of the room.

She could smell *something* that made her already ravenous belly groan with desire. She followed the scent through the house. She couldn't quite figure out where it came from and only knew she wanted it. Finally, finding herself at the front door, she frowned for a moment as she realized the closer she got, the more she could smell it. Getting on hands and knees, she put her face along a crack at the bottom and breathed deeply, inhaling as much of the intoxicating scent as she could. From here, she could hear noises coming from outside getting closer.

Curious, she stood up to try to see out the window just as the door flew open, pushing her backwards. Suddenly, The Smell was overwhelming, and she looked and saw several people standing in front of her, their stances aggressive. The Smell was coming from them and it made her hungry, and angry. Working purely on instinct, she growled and jumped up, and started running towards them.

Before she made it out the door, something poked her neck, and everything went black.

"How many more do you think we need?" The woman asked as she lit a cigarette, inhaling deeply.

"We have half a dozen in the back already, as well as the ones we already have back at base. Surely that's enough for now?"

The man beside her focused on the road ahead and didn't respond immediately.

"Yo, Johnson! How many more?" She finally shouted impatiently.

Specialist Chris Johnson did not like Morgan. He found her crass, rude and entirely unlikable. He preferred that feminine woman were seen and not heard. But at the end of the world, you didn't exactly get to choose the people you were teamed up with.

The two of them had been tasked with rounding up a handful of zombies from various areas outside of their new base located just outside of Vancouver. They had driven around for a while, surveying the surrounding area, before picking a random suburban neighborhood. They had gone through several blocks of houses that were empty, filled with corpses, or were unsuitable for a number of other reasons before coming across the blonde one they had just picked up.

Their newly appointment captain, Jeffery Wolfe, had a team of scientists at his disposal and had plans for this group in the back. What those experiments entailed varied and Chris preferred to stay out of it.

"We'll bring them back to base for now and wrangle up some more if we need to. I'm done being out here. It's fucking depressing," he responded tersely.

For a few moments, the only noises were the angry cries and groans coming from the back of the van.

Clawing, howling, yelling.

Chris gripped the wheel tighter, clenching his teeth in annoyance. "Be quiet back there!" he yelled, and was rewarded with an even louder response while Morgan laughed at his anger.

"Dude, they are zombies. They can't fucking understand you," she smirked.

He flipped Morgan off and turned on a CD, turning it up as loud as it would go. The music blasted, drowning out the noises in the back.

"It's the end of the world as we know it, and I feel fine..."

CHAPTER 6

"What's your name, anyway?" the boy asked, sitting with his back against the bathroom door. Max sat on the opposite side in the same position. He thought about it for a minute.

"Don't know," Max responded sadly.

The boy contemplated this for a moment. He imagined that would have been a very confusing and lonely way to wake up. He felt for the man, wondering if he truly understood the situation.

"You do know..." the boy hesitated, "you do know you are dead right? Like...I don't want to offend you, man, but you do know that, right?"

"What mean dead?" Max replied, recognizing the word but wanting to be sure he was understanding.

"Well," the boy paused again, "it's like, you died. Kinda like you went to sleep forever but got back up again."

"Oh." Max did remember waking up. *I am dead?*

The silence between them was deafening, and immediately the boy felt bad for bringing it up. Max wasn't offended though, just melancholy over his forgetfulness. Being dead wasn't all that bad, but not being able to remember how to do or say things brought a feeling of loss he didn't like.

"Name?" Max asked finally, trying to get the conversation going again. He liked talking to the youth. He felt like the more he was around someone, even just through a door, the more pieces of himself kept fitting together. He didn't want to lose that again.

"I'm Jason. But my friends call me Jay or Jay-man," he responded proudly.

Max grinned. "Jay-man."

"We should make a name for you too. You know, just until you can remember better."

Jay thought about it for a moment. "I know! How about Daryl? He was like, my favorite character on this rad show about zombies...."

The boy continued talking, but Max didn't hear anything after that.

Zombie.

That word he remembered quickly. Is that what he was? Max vaguely remembered zombies as fearsome monsters who killed and ate people. Brainless, terrifying, and evil were all words his mind conjured when he considered the word 'Zombie.'

Jay's reaction when he first came into the room made a lot more sense now. Right now, he didn't feel violent, didn't feel like killing people. However, he did remember The Smell that came off Jay when he first came in. It had made him feel angry. And hungry. Then again, he could still smell it; it just wasn't driving him into an anxious frenzy like before.

"...but then the show got kind of lame, so I stopped watching it. Hey man, are you listening? What do you think? Is Daryl a good name?" Jay prattled on.

"Jay-man. Me Daryl," He replied sullenly.

For a moment, Jay was silent.

"Did I say something wro…" before Jay could finish the sentence, he felt an overwhelming sense of nausea and barely made it to the toilet before his stomach emptied itself of the meager bits he had been feeding it the past days. He continued to heave and sputter, his head spinning like a top.

On the other side of the door Max listened, concerned. "Jay, you okay? What wrong?"

Jay continued to heave and spit on the other side of the door. Max rattled the doorknob, once again frustrated at another doorknob keeping him out.

"Open…I help."

Jay wiped his mouth and sat against the bathtub.

"Daryl…You seem real nice and all. Especially for a zombie. But how do I know you aren't going to try to eat me?" Jay replied, not wanting to offend him but was unsure if he could bring himself to ignore the basic instinct which had led him to the bathroom in the first place.

Max thought about this for a second, pressing his forehead against the door. He wanted to help, felt an odd sense of care over Jay, but he knew there were no reassurances he could give the boy, or even himself.

After all, he was a zombie, wasn't he?

For the rest of the day, Jay spoke to Max, telling him stories of before FIRE hit. He spoke about his parents, his friends, and even spent a good half hour talking about the little girl, Dawn, who had lived next to him. He told Max she was like an annoying kid sister, but he missed her and wondered where she was now.

Max was pleased that, throughout the day, more words were coming back to him to the point that he could respond in mostly full sentences, with the only major difference being the strange new cadence in his voice.

By that evening Jay was getting worse. Max listened and stayed by the door but was unable to do anything to help his new friend. A familiar feeling of hopelessness settled over Max as he listened to Jay empty his body again and again. Max listened to him cough and sputter, the racking sobs clear even through the door.

It seemed to Max that he had a history involving this feeling of helplessness, and the inability to remember why further depressed him.

"Jay," he asked, "I help you?"

There was silence on the other side of the door.

One minute went by.

Two.

For a moment, Max worried the boy had already died and that he would never be able to get to him or talk to anyone again. He wasn't entirely sure which was worse.

Finally, the teen responded, and Max sighed in relief.

"No, Daryl," Jay said through gritted teeth. His body felt like a furnace, starting from the bite in his arm and spreading all through his limbs.

"Daryl, I think…I think I'm infected."

Max paced the room for a while, those words repeating on a loop through his head.

I'm infected, Jay had said. Or he said he thought he was infected.

Cursing his slow brain, Max tried to work through what this meant.

It means he will probably die, he told himself as he stopped pacing. *It means he will be like me.* A guilty feeling of the thought of relieving his own loneliness crossed his mind.

Max continued his pacing and trying to force his thoughts into completion.

When Jay came in the room, he thought. *No that isn't right…Wait…He opened the door to the room….*

The door!

The fucking doorknob of hell!

Max rushed back over to the door.

"Jay…Jay-man!!" His words rushed out of him as he banged on the door to get the boy's attention.

Groaning, but without opening his eyes or moving from his spot on the floor, Jay snapped, "What?"

Jay felt a twinge of guilt at how sharp that word had sounded, but in all honesty, he felt awful. He couldn't open his eyes without shooting pains piercing his brain. He had thrown up and soiled himself almost a dozen times, sometimes both at once. Every movement hurt.

He coughed lightly, which brought another sharp pain, and tried again a bit softer.

"What is it, Daryl?" he tried again, softer this time.

Max explained quickly to the boy what he had been thinking.

"Jay-man…You sick. Know me can't help…Me not even help me." He stopped for a moment. "I know you don't trust yet and don't know what can do convince you. But you need know a thing."

Max stopped again for effect. "If Jay-man die and don't open this…Fucking door, then you trapped in there…Like Daryl. And it sucks." He finally finished, proud at himself for getting those words out in what he hoped was a coherent way.

Jay sat up a little higher, listening to the words as he thought about this.

Although they hadn't talked about it before, it did make sense as to why he was just sitting in a hotel room. The key controlled door had been unlocked and yet, Daryl truly didn't know how to get out. Jay had come bursting through the door not expecting to see anyone, or anything, on the other side.

"Please, Jay-man, open door… And other door, before in case of you die," Max continued, with zero subtlety.

For a long time, they both waited. Max wondered if maybe he could even figure out the doorknob if only someone showed him once. He figured out words that way, didn't he?

Meanwhile, Jay took inventory over his body and its various aches again. Like a looped mantra in his head, he went from toe to head, noting to himself the things that hurt. *Toes feel kind of numb, but my knee is burning hot. My chest feels heavy and full. My arm is kind of numb and hot too….* Tears welled in his eyes as he accepted his fate. He was going to die. Jay knew from the news that he had about a one in three chance of waking up again.

As his tears fell, he thought about his new acquaintance, Daryl. He had never heard of nice zombies before. Or even talking ones for that matter. But there had been that awful growl when he first came barreling into the room. And the others that had been chasing him, leading to room 1201.

When I first came into the room, Daryl was more zombie than he is now. Maybe when I turn into a zombie, he can teach me how to not be like those…things. Or maybe I'll just stay dead, but at least if I die I will have helped Daryl get out.

Although it hurt, he wiped his tears away angrily and struggled to stand up. With determination, he put his hand on the door handle and turned.

CHAPTER 7

Clara woke up confined, with blackness filling her vision and a steady low rumbling beneath her. Flailing about, she quickly found she had been gagged, and there was fabric covering her head, blocking her sight. Disoriented, she tried to move her arms only to realize that they too were bound. She tossed her head back and forth in a frenzy until the sack covering it slipped off, revealing a dimly lit area with several people around her who were similarly bound.

Across from her was another woman who had managed to remove the bag. The rest remained covered, snarls and growls coming from beneath some of the bags. Clara noticed that most of the others also had visible injuries that looked like bite marks. She wondered if someone as hungry as her had taken a bite....

She stopped moving as she looked at the other woman's face with interest. She had lanky brown hair and skin that looked like it was once darker, but now had the appearance of coffee with too much cream. Even in the minimal lighting, Clara could tell the woman's eyes were unnaturally pale blue.

The other woman nodded her head towards the barrier separating them from the noise and made a small sound in her throat as she shook her head.

Clara frowned, unsure of what to make of this. She felt like she should be able to respond somehow, but words failed her, and she started to let out a groan of her own but quickly stopped at another head shake.

Clara's frown deepened as she took in more of her surroundings.

There were six of them total, all bound in a small space that bumped and vibrated.

Van.

The word fluttered through her mind. Behind the other woman was a wall, and Clara could hear music drifting through the tight area.

She also smelled The Smell drifting in from the front. The Smell that made her want to rip and tear and...Eat.

Her confusion quickly turned back to anger. She howled loudly beneath her gag and started wrestling against the bonds that tied her. The other woman kept shaking her head, her eyes wide, looking between Clara and the front of the van, but stayed silent as she watched Clara struggle.

After a few minutes, Clara realized she would not get free this way, as she assumed the others had discovered earlier based on their current stillness, and ceased struggling. She laid back and tried to get comfortable while the music blared around them.

After what seemed like a long time, the vibrating stopped, along with the music. The others around her all started thrashing about again, irritated by the change. One more bag fell off from another one who didn't have visible bite marks and revealed an older man. Spittle dribbled down his chin through the gag and anger flared in his eyes. Clara felt no fear, but rather sensed a kindred spirit. As soon as he caught her eye he stopped for a moment, taking her in as she did the same.

He nodded in acknowledgement after a few silent moments. Before Clara could nod back, they all whipped their heads towards the loud slam of a door coming from the front of the van. Footsteps crunched on gravel, and the three without bags followed the sound until it led them to the closed doors.

In a flurry, the van doors opened, and angry shouting began as all six were unceremoniously pulled out and thrown onto the rocks. In front of them was a large building with a door covered in strange symbols that Clara knew meant *something*.

She growled as she looked up at two people she recognized from earlier in the day. One of them, a woman, laughed and kicked at her side while pulling something out of her pocket and putting it to her mouth.

"Look at the dumb zombie, thinks she's gonna get free," the woman laughed as she lit her cigarette. Clara couldn't quite understand the words, but even in her current form she felt the mockery and glared at the woman. The man beside her scowled and leaned down and picked her up by her bound hands. He held her steady at arm's length.

Several other people came running out and began picking up the others, leading them all towards the double doors in front of them.

For the first time since her death, Clara felt a twinge of fear as she was led through the heavy doors with her new companions.

They emerged at the start of a long hallway, fluorescent lights glaring off the white walls. Several men stood at the inside of the doors with black metal in their hands. She immediately recognized them as a threat and growled at them. Then she felt a prick of pressure on her neck and everything went dark again.

Clara woke up no longer bound or gagged. Noises of aggression and, strangely, laughter, fluttered through the air. Opening her eyes, she found herself in a large metal cage, the fluorescent lights replaced with dim flickering bulbs. She sat up to take in more of her surroundings.

There were maybe two dozen others inside the cage with her, most of whom were mulling around aimlessly or sitting. On the opposite wall from the fence were a few rows of boxes, piled almost to the ceiling. There were no windows in the entire room and the area felt cool and slightly damp.

A few people inside the cage aggressively shook the metal links, howling and screaming at the men on the other side who sat laughing with their guns in hand. Although she didn't know the others, she felt upset at the blatant mockery. Ignoring that for now, she looked around again and noticed the woman she had been bound in the van with sitting a few feet away from her, leaning against a wall. The woman gave Clara a small nod and patted the area on the floor next to her. For lack of a better option, Clara went and joined her, and they sat in silence.

She must have dozed off for a while, and awoke suddenly to someone gently shaking her.

"Pssfftt."

Clara groaned as she opened her eyes to see who had shaken her. She immediately noticed that the cage was almost silent and the only man on the other side appeared to be asleep.

"Pssffft," the woman said again, and Clara finally met her eyes.

"You understand me?" the woman whispered.

Clara looked at her blankly for a moment as the words registered. She felt slow, sluggish, but a vague comprehension was there. She nodded at the woman.

"Not all us remember," the woman continued whispering. "Some take longer than others, some don't think ever will…. But can't let *Them* know that we do." She indicated the snoring man outside the cage.

Clara frowned at this, frustrated by the time it was taking her brain to process. "The words will come back," the woman kept on, keeping her voice low. "Give time and you see."

Clara sighed and nodded again.

"The word for this," the woman whispered, showing a nod, "is yes."

The word stuck, and Clara smiled. "Yass," she replied, happy to have at least one word. The woman shushed her again but smiled back at her and Clara was struck by how white and shiny her teeth were. They seemed to glow against the light mocha colour of her skin, and her smile gave Clara a feeling of comfort.

The woman pointed to the other end of the cage where the grey-haired man from the van sat. He leaned casually, arms over his knees, as he looked around, taking in everything around him. When he met Clara's eyes he nodded again and continued his watch.

"He remembers too," the woman said quietly, leaning back and closing her eyes. They sat together in silence for the rest of the night.

CHAPTER 8

Max stood only two feet in front of the door, excited yet nervous as he realized that the boy was in fact coming out. Though he could still sense The Smell coming from under the door, he felt a level of control that had come back with the words. He was still anxious but felt confident he wouldn't harm Jay.

Max watched as the door swung open, and he didn't move or speak for a moment, trying to get a better look at his new young friend. He could tell Jay was afraid, but even sick as he was, Max was sure he was doing his best to stand tall and meet his own steady gaze. He felt a strange surge of pride for the youth before taking in the rest of his appearance.

Jay does not look good, Max thought as he looked over his flushed but pale skin, and then the angry red bite on his arm. The smell emanating from Jay was slightly stronger now with the door open, but incredibly faint compared to when he had first entered the room. Max wondered what that meant.

Smiling in what he hoped was a non-threatening way, Max held out his hand in offering, hoping for Jay's sake that he would take it. After only a couple second delay Jay took his hand and let himself be led out of the bathroom. Max could feel Jay begin to stumble and quickly helped him over to the bed. Although it was stained and filthy, not to mention ripped into pieces, Jay seemed to hardly notice as he sat down. He put his head into his hands.

"Daryl…did you go through this too?" Jay asked quietly.

Max hesitated for a moment. What happened to him was a question he had obsessed over in the first few days of his imprisonment.

Flashes of pain, heat, loneliness. Black voids between now and before. Worry. A sense of loss. Max shuttered slightly at the recollection, willing those memories to stay gone.

"I do remember bits. It strange…Like there is fog in my brain that clears up some parts but stays dark others," Max finally replied, proud at being able to articulate himself better than before.

"I feel like there is something I need to know. That I'm forgetting. I just don't know. I don't remember before here and it's driving me crazy. Couldn't talk until heard you. I just feel…slow." Max finished lamely.

Jay sat for a moment, lost in thought about these revelations.

"It fits with what I was thinking earlier," Jay finally replied. "When I first came in here you were more…zombie. You're actually not too bad now that I've gotten to know you."

Max smiled a bit sadly.

"It was your smell too," Max admitted reluctantly. "That what made me so…angry. You still smell a little but it is a lot less…. Before it just made me so…hungry."

Max turned away, ashamed to admit he wanted to eat his new friend.

Jay startled a bit at Max's realization, but it wasn't really shocking. He supposed that zombies smelling people wasn't the weirdest revelation of the day. It was then that Jay looked down at the bite and realized it had stopped throbbing at some point, though it was still an angry red. He didn't think that was a good sign.

"Well, I should open the door now. Come on, let me show you," Jay said, avoiding thoughts of his injury. He slowly shambled towards the door, holding his hurt arm close to his chest. Turning the knob, he slowly pulled the door open, listening for any sounds in the corridor. Silence greeted him and he opened it the rest of the way before turning to Max, who was staring intently at his hand and the doorknob.

"Stupid…fucking thing," Max muttered as he glared at it, causing Jay to laugh.

"Why don't you try it," Jay said, still laughing lightly as he quietly shut the door.

Max inhaled and looked at his hand, willing it to do what Jay's had done. Slowly, his body complied, and he reached towards the lever and twisted before letting go. It sprang back into place. The door remained closed. Max gnashed his teeth as he tried again, this time leaning his hand into the door more so he wouldn't let go.

He was rewarded with a click as the door cracked open, and he grinned.

"Did it!" he declared happily.

Jay smiled wearily and started shuffling back towards the bed. Finally looking down at the state of the sheets, Jay sighed, but was so tired he was prepared to lie down regardless. He wondered if Daryl would leave him now that he could get out.

Max quickly figured out the reason behind Jay's sigh. "Wait!" he cried just before Jay could lay down.

"Let me…" Max yanked off the remaining shreds of fabric, exposed the relatively clean mattress. Jay smiled and laid down directly, not caring about the lack of sheets or pillows, appreciating the effort and the idea of being horizontal.

"Thanks Dary—" he started to say before he erupted in a coughing fit so strong he vomited all over one side of the bed. *So much for that,* Jay thought as his head spun and he shifted over a few inches away from the mess.

Max looked on helplessly, unsure of what to do to help. Suddenly he was struck by a vague memory; more of a feeling, really. A feeling of being helpless, of wanting to make something better but not being able to. The feeling of a failure.

Shaking the melancholy thoughts away, he focused on the now.

"Jay-man, what can I do?" Max asked quietly now that the boy had finished retching. Breathing heavily but still lying on his side, he twisted around to look up at Max. "Well…I don't know if I can keep it down, but can you try to find me some food? I've been drinking water in the bathroom, but I am mighty hungry."

Max visibly brightened at the idea that he could do something to help. "Sure. Yes. Okay. Umm…what does food look like? I mean…only thing that smells like 'to eat' I don't think you want and I already ate what I could find in here," Max joked. Jay smiled a bit at that.

"Yeah, don't think I'm quite up for that…Just…maybe check that fridge for a start," Jay responded, pointing to the small mini fridge under the desk opposite the bed.

Max immediately stood up and went over it, staring blankly for a moment. Jay quickly realized the problem.

"On the side of it. No, the other side. Just pull it up a bit towards you, kind of like the door."

He managed to pull it open and found a few small packages and bottles which he brought over to the bed. Jay lifted his head enough to look through the findings.

"Well, I think I'll pass on the whiskey for now, but these nuts and chips will do," he said picking through the items.

"Whiskey?" Max questioned.

"Well, I'm only like fourteen, man…. I mean, I've stolen a few beers from my parents' fridge before…." Jay stopped, gulping a bit as he thought of his parents again. He had just left them there….

Max noticed the change in mood but couldn't quite grasp why. He frowned, about to ask, but was interrupted by Jay's outpouring of words.

"My parents…they…died. I left them. Just ran as fast and as far as I could," Jay sputtered, tears welling in his eyes.

"I should have helped them. Done more. But they were so sick. Like I am now." The tears began to fall in earnest.

"After I left I was by myself for a few days, I think. It's funny that a few weeks ago I would have loved to have the freedom to do what I wanted. I always hated rules and having a curfew, going to school. But now, I just miss them," he finished sadly.

Max didn't quite know what to say. Even as a zombie, he did understand the feeling of loss, even if he still wasn't sure what it was that he had lost. He looked down at the band on his finger once again, absently rubbing it while he watched Jay eat.

<hr />

It was getting late, and for the last few hours Jay had progressively gotten worse. With no sheets and excrement and vomit coming out of both ends of him, Jay now sat on saturated bed. Since Max didn't register the smell as being bad, he didn't even think to do anything about it this time. Jay was essentially beyond noticing at this point, and certainly beyond caring.

"Hey Daryl," Jay finally said in a quiet voice.

"Yeah, Jay-Man?"

"I have an idea.... Do you have a bag around here or something?"

Max looked around the dim room and found the item he thought Jay was talking about, proud at himself for recognizing the word. He held it up to confirm it was what the boy meant. Jay nodded.

"Look for a little folded thing. It's called a wallet. You could have some ID or something in there. I didn't think of this before, but at least before I die we can figure out your real name."

Max frowned at this. "Jay-man, it not for sure that you're gonna...."

The boy erupted into another coughing fit. When he finally finished he held his hand out, staring into Max's eyes firmly. Max stared back sadly, noting a glazed look under the determination that hadn't been there before. He dug through the bag until he found the item. Since he didn't know what to do with it, he held it out to Jay for direction.

With a bit of difficulty, Jay sat up on the bed and took the wallet. He flipped through for a moment, stopping on something before looking up at Max and hesitating. After a moment, he flipped again and pulled out a small piece of plastic.

"Maxwell Alan Jacobs of Vancouver, British Columbia," Jay read with surprise. "Wow, Daryl...I mean, Max...That's like, on the other side of the country. What are you doing in Toronto?"

Max smiled at hearing his given name.

Max.

That sounded right. And while he didn't know where Vancouver or Toronto were, both words rang bells in his head.

"Don't know," he admitted. "But thank you…for finding out name. It feels good to know."

Jay smiled a bit warily. He debated for a moment whether to show Max the other thing he had found in the wallet. Finally, he flipped it back and pulled out a photo and handed it to Max.

Unsure, Max reached out to take it from his hand. It was a photo of him! But not as pale looking, and he was with…he was with…All of a sudden, Max's memories began flooding back.

"Clara…."

CHAPTER 9

Rachel Samborski was one of the few people in the world still alive who had been studying the virus since the start, trying to find a cure. Before air traffic stopped, she had been transported to a medical facility just outside of Seattle to continue her work and was allowed a small team. From there, they kept analyzing the virus until it stopped being considered just a particularly bad infectious virus and the focus of their research was forced to change. Now, the word on everyone's mind was simply "Zombies."

North America was hit hard and fast with the virus, as was the rest of the world. Speculation was that it originated in India; however, that was up for debate. It happened so quickly that it was difficult to pinpoint any true starting point. By the time the first death in Delhi was reported, the first infections were being noticed in New York.

Both the US and Canadian governments were no longer functioning, or at least no longer able to do anything to help their citizens. Borders meant nothing, and there were few places that were safe.

When things started getting crazier, Rachel and her team were escorted north into Canada along with several "live specimens" they had obtained to continue her research. Just outside of Vancouver, Rachel performed her research in a military facility that, while basic, suited their needs for a rudimentary lab and containment area.

During the ride up, almost half of the soldiers that had come along had been killed, as well as several of the scientists. By the time they arrived, the highest-ranking person alive was Jeffrey Wolfe, a captain with a reputation for cruelty that surpassed even his predecessor, which was a feat in itself.

The remaining scientists, led by Rachel, had been tasked with finding out more about the infected—what their weaknesses were as well as how to fight the virus. When Wolfe had given her the instructions, she got the feeling the cure was less important to him than finding out better ways to fight them.

She also had suspicions about the other experiments that were not happening under her supervision, but hadn't had the time or resources to prove anything.

The specimens who had gotten up again after death were typically incredibly aggressive, and careful handling was required. Some seemed far more sedated though, but it was difficult to determine on sight alone.

Their research so far was nothing short of astounding, and it was Rachel's job as head of the small team to deliver the information to Captain Wolfe, as well as several other high-ranking officials who remained. Despite the lack of government, these men were very much in charge. It was a meeting she was not looking forward to.

———

"At this point we have confirmed that the virus, dubbed FIRE, is highly infectious and airborne. We can only assume people like ourselves are immune as we have obviously been exposed. About 95% of those exposed do contract a form of the virus, and of those infected about 75% die, usually due to encephalitis and incredible high fever. The real curiosity here is that approximately 30% of those who have died have apparently risen from the dead." Rachel paused for a moment, confirming she had her audience's attention.

"The subjects who die and get up again are, in fact, alive once more, but altered. This phenomenon is sometimes known as the Lazarus effect or syndrome. To clarify, when these patients wake up, they are alive once more. These are not 'walking dead.' We believe it is a combination of total organ failure, the hypoxic ischemic encephalopathy, and the high fever that causes the subjects to lose so much brain function. We have also found that several specific areas of the brain are damaged when the virus is contracted, including the ventromedial frontal cortex. This is a part of the brain associated with reactive aggression, such as the behavior we have seen in the subjects. The periaqueductal gray area is also affected, which, in a way, turns off pain sensors, meaning that those infected will have reduced response to pain and physical stimuli." Another pause, noticing a few faces that had glazed over at some of the words used. Clearing her throat, she tried to summarize.

"This loss of brain function reverts their instincts back to the absolute basics, such as hunger. They feel little pain and they seem to have difficulty identifying and opening most manmade food products but respond best to meat. Their bodies don't seem to require as much sustenance as before, with many of them going days without eating, and seem to desire protein. They direct their hunger on humans who are, to put it crudely, a fresh source of meat. There may be some smell factor as well, as we can see strange stimulation in their brains which seems to increase when non-infected humans are present," she continued.

"In conclusion, the subjects we call 'zombies' are not, in fact, dead, and are rather brain damaged people who have survived infection with the side effects of heightened aggression and lowered intelligence. They are simply people who have recovered from the infection with a severe, but stable, mania. In some cases of encephalitis such as this, people are known to recover some brain function over time. Within 8 to 12 months we will have a better idea of the maximum capacity, but it is my belief we can improve outcomes through rehab...." She trailed off, taking in the looks she was now receiving.

Around the room, people stared at her with expressions varying from confusion, to disbelief, to outright anger. That last one she didn't quite understand.

Laughter floated from one corner of the room, where Captain Wolfe had been leaning against the wall with an angry sort of smirk on his face.

"Whether they are dead now or not, they are vicious killers and a threat. You're talking about, what? Treating zombies? Zombie therapy?" Wolfe finished on another laugh. Several others joined in with him.

Rachel frowned at this reaction, crossing her arms over her chest.

"Whatever you may think, this means they are still people," she retorted. "If we can help them, we should."

Wolfe walked forward to address the room. His confident swagger immediately put Rachel on edge. To her, he seemed more like an animal than a man, trying to demonstrate his superiority and dominance. She thought back to a program she had once watched on National Geographic about predators and establishing dominance. It was this posture she was seeing now.

"I don't know how many of you have been out there recently, but it's the bloody apocalypse. People are dying and coming back, attacking other people. There is only one appropriate response to this situation, and it is not," Captain Wolfe stopped for a moment, shooting a glare in Rachel's direction, "*teaching* the fucking things."

Around them conversation erupted as people stopped to discuss the implications of Captain Wolfe's words. From the bits that Rachel was hearing, the overwhelming majority seemed to agree with his speech.

"Dr. Samborski," he finally said, halting all other conversation in the room, "please continue your research. We need to know more about what we are dealing with. However, in the meantime, anyone showing signs of aggression or attacking others will be dealt with accordingly...whether they are *alive* or not."

———————

Downstairs, Clara sat with her new friends while those around them slept. It had been two days since they were placed into the metal cage, and since then the humans outside of it were vigilant in keeping watch other than the few moments on the first day when the single guard had fallen asleep.

This was the first time they had been left completely alone since then, and while they welcomed the opportunity to speak to one another, there was a certain wariness among the group.

During this time, unable to test her new understanding of speech, Clara listened to the advice of her new friends.

So she watched, and she listened.

Meaningful glances had been exchanged between her and some of the others, but it was also apparent that not all those among them had any remaining comprehension. She looked upon them with something akin to pity.

The light bulbs overhead buzzed and flickered, casting a somewhat ominous glow on the three as they congregated on one side of the cage. There was one other man who sat close by, apparently listening, but seemingly not entirely present either.

"Seventeen here tells me you can understand," the grey-haired man said to Clara. It was not so much a question as a statement of what he believed.

Clara nodded in return, somehow nervous about trying speech for herself.

"Y-yes," she replied simply a moment later, pleased with herself for the clarity of her voice.

The grey-haired man nodded towards the one who was listening.

"This is Nine. He understands a bit but can't speak"

Clara turned to Nine and nodded in greeting. Although he looked back at her, his stare was absent, and he grunted in reply but didn't say anything further.

"Do you remember what you are called? Your name?" Seventeen, her dark-skinned friend, asked her. Clara thought for a moment. Although she understood the question, she didn't know the answer. While words were coming back to her, memory of anything before waking up in the house was still fuzzy. Without being obvious about it, she reached her hand into her robe to assure herself the picture was still there.

"No, do you?" Clara asked as she subtly stroked the picture in her pocket.

The woman shook her head on behalf of both of them.

"No, we don't either. We were both taken many days ago. We were being sent here when you were picked up. But in the other place, they called me

Seventeen and him Three. I don't think those were our before names, though." Seventeen shrugged. "I don't mind. Until I remember more, I don't care what I am called."

Clara could understand that sentiment. She also wished to remember more.

Walking through the house after she woke up, she had felt vague parts of memories but couldn't pinpoint them with any accuracy. But really, she mostly wanted to remember who the man in the picture was. For a moment, she debated showing Three and Seventeen the picture, but for some reason hesitated. He was just for her, at least for now.

"Where were you before?" Clara asked, changing the subject and gesturing to the cage around them. Hesitation from both of her new friends.

Seventeen was visibly upset at the question and stood up and paced a bit. The behavior worried Clara, and she turned to Three, a small crease in her brow.

"We don't know where it was," Three began haltingly. "But it was much darker than here. There started off being about this many of us," he gestured around the cage, "but by the time we left only a small number of us remained, including me, Seventeen, and Nine here. They would take us away one by one. We heard… " he trailed off as though trying to formulate the words, but Seventeen picked up the conversation, anger in her eyes and voice.

"There was screaming. Not like these dummies do when they are upset," she pointed at the sleeping forms around them. "They were hurt. On purpose. By *them*!" Three stood up and put a hand on her shoulder, and she immediately visibly deflated.

"Seventeen has been through a lot already. We tell you more in time, but for now know that in the place before, the ones who spoke or showed they were smarter…well, they weren't in the van with us. And that is why you shouldn't speak around *Them*."

CHAPTER 10

Silence greeted them when they first walked into the hall, although Max had grinned to himself when he opened the door with ease. They wandered down the corridor, not quite creeping, but keeping a slow pace. Up ahead a few noises could be heard, although it wasn't yet obvious what they were.

Frowning, Max looked back at Jay, who stood closely behind him as if waiting for further instruction. While Jay had woken up, he had yet to communicate beyond the occasional grunt, and had a slightly glazed over look in his eyes that hadn't faded. Max was delighted that he had woken up at all.

While receptive to basic commands and needs, he was still in that familiar fog that Max himself had experienced until only a few days before and did not miss. Even though Max didn't know if the boy could totally understand, he explained to him that they needed to leave. They had no food there, and they needed to find Clara. He showed Jay the picture from his wallet by way of explanation. Jay seemed to understand what food was and quickly followed Max after that.

Max had high hopes that, like his own recovery, he would regain more of himself in the coming days. He thought back to the days after he woke up and the haze that had clouded his brain, and how it was Jay's words that really set the switch to bring words back to the front of his brain. He had tried speaking to Jay in the room, but had not received any responses, and barely any recognition at all until the mention of food.

Remembering back to the food under the tray when Max first woke up, he decided they should see if they could find some food in the building before leaving. While practical, there was also a part of Max that was afraid of what they might find in the outside world. As much as he had hated being stuck in that room, with that stupid doorknob, this place was all he knew of the world outside his still-foggy memories.

Walking to the top of the stairs, Max looked down to survey the area. On the carpeted landing below, there was an infected man sitting and leaning against the wall, eating the last scraps of a body he had clearly liberated at some point earlier. The faint but familiar smell of the uninfected living still hung heavy in the air along with the metallic scent of blood.

Slowly, but with a sense of purpose, the infected man got up and started walking up the stairs towards them, blood dripping off his chin as he grinned at the two newcomers. Max took a step back instinctively, putting his arm and body out in front of Jay, who looked at the other infected with curiosity. As the bloody man walked up the stairs towards them, Max felt an angry possessive feeling come over him.

Who the fuck does this guy think he is trying to intimidate me, Max thought as he unconsciously planted his feet and opened his shoulders and body. Growling slightly, he addressed the now-stopped zombie in front of them.

"Fuck off whadyawant," Max growled at him.

Cowed by the domineering approach, the man immediately stared at the ground and hunched down in fear and shame. Seeing this exchange, Jay walked around him, keeping a distance, but obviously curious about the body in the corner. Max remembered The Smell, faint but true, emanating from the corpse and immediately understood the desires that Jay was feeling.

"Jay-man, wait," Max said, stopping the boy before he reached the corpse. Turning his attention back to the infected man in front of him, he resumed his growl and increased a few decibels.

"Go. NOW!" Max shouted, causing the man to scramble down the stairs, almost tripping on his feet as he exited through the doors at the back of the lobby. He watched him leave before approaching Jay slowly. Max honestly didn't really know what to say or feel in that moment.

The last week or so of being a zombie, or whatever he was, and in particular the last thirty-six hours waiting with Jay, had given him enough time to notice the differences between first waking up and now. In particular, memories of being…not this.

While still a bit physically slow, and even though he couldn't remember a lot of his life, he was starting to recall overall concepts like social structure. Max also knew that before this, he hadn't been tempted to eat people, and the vaguest idea of this being wrong stayed his head. The idea of guilt, as opposed to the actual emotion, plagued his mind.

Max looked at Jay and remembered how he had savored and craved that scent when he was first locked up. The scent that Max hadn't understood at the time he now knew to be uninfected people. It was the smell of hot, live blood and flesh, and of pure, uninfected brain. It was almost euphoric, and even now Max could feel that familiar pull, although he was capable of resisting it.

Trying to break it down logically, he looked down at the very, *very* dead body in front of them. Clothes were ripped and torn to shreds to make easy access and looking down he thought he could see the dead man's heart through a missing piece of his ribs.

This person is already dead, Max reasoned with himself. *We didn't kill him. He won't be any less dead for us having a few bites. I'm just getting us a good meal for the road.*

Smiling to himself for thinking of it, he looked around once more to ensure there were no more visitors and then extended an arm in front of him, inviting Jay to dinner.

"Okay zombie Jay-man," Max said, "eat up."

Jay practically pounced on the remains, obviously famished. Max hung back for a moment, intending to let the boy have first dibs. Just as he began leaning down to take a taste of the tantalizing meal in front of him, he heard a commotion down the hallway coming from the direction the bloody man had run. Instructing Jay to stay put, he walked down the hall to investigate.

While Jay had been ill he had watched out of the window and, based on the awkward movements, he could now deduce which people below were infected like himself. Pale skin seemed to be the easiest distinguishing factor, plus the infected tended to be slower and less coordinated. From what he had seen so far, they were also generally more laid back and not as aggressive compared to what he was hearing from down the hall.

Turning down the corridor, he saw the bloody fiend he had just chased off along with two others pounding on a doorway. He could hear noises coming from the other side as he got closer. The group saw Max coming, but seeing his alabaster skin they quickly ignored him. The one he had scared off earlier stared at Max momentarily, unsure if he was about to be run off from yet another meal. He quickly turned his attention back to the door once he realized Max was merely watching them.

Whimpers and cries came from the other side and the noises immediately struck deep in Max's heart, causing it to pound. Even though Max didn't know how he knew, he could tell the noises were from a child. The first instinct he had was what he knew was driving the others into a frenzy; *The Smell*, combined with those noises, indicated that a meal was on the other side.

Max's humanity was recovering along with his memories, and sorrow filled him as he listened to the child's obvious struggles and fear. It didn't take him long to decide what to do, and he quickly recalled the reaction of the infected man when he had taken a dominating approach earlier.

Puffing up his chest and putting on the most intimidating face he could muster, he started stomping down the hall towards them. "Mine!" he yelled as the halls shook with the force of his steps. His old 'friend' quickly ran off the other way, leaving the other two behind. The remaining infected were a man and a woman who had paused their assault on the door at Max's approach, taking a slight step back.

After a moment, the man growled, stepping forward to challenge Max. Even though Max was not expecting this, he held his ground, continuing his loud approach, determined that the child would be his.

The other infected man rushed towards him, and Max immediately noticed the disjointed, awkward movements which indicated the man was recently turned. Max dug his feet in and growled, preparing for the attack. Once a few feet away, the infected man stopped, still growling at Max, who didn't flinch or move but instead remained steady and solid in the center of the hallway. His eyes narrowed at his opponent and the steady low growl stayed in his throat. The woman behind him looked on with curiosity.

"This. One. Mine." Max repeated, calmly but sternly.

Before he could say any more, the man rushed towards him, tackling Max. Seeing him go down, the woman immediately started shambling over towards them. The two men grappled on the ground and, while the other infected man was slightly bigger, Max was obviously the more coordinated of the two. Punching the other man in the face, Max stunned his opponent and rolled up, preparing himself for the female to hit.

With zero finesse, she ran towards him. Max saw his opportunity and decked her so hard she fell to the floor, dazed for the moment. As the other man began to rise, Max's instincts took over as he growled and jumped on him, hitting him again and again. Time lost meaning as he continued his assault, the absence of pain giving him no indication that he needed to stop.

Over and over Max kept punching the man's head, pulverizing it until it was no longer recognizable as a face. Blood and offal covered Max, and his chest heaved as he sat on the other now *very* dead man. He looked up and realized the woman had run away at some point during the one-sided brawl. His knuckles gleamed with redness.

It took a moment for his senses to come back, and he noticed the small noises coming from the door had stopped except for a few very quiet whimpers. Wiping his arm across his face, Max stood up.

He walked up to the door tentatively, not quite sure how to handle the situation from here. He looked around, and when he didn't hear or see anyone else, he knocked quietly on the door. The whimpers stopped. "Hello?" a small girlish voice asked through the door.

"Hello. I chase off other guys," he started, unsure of what to say. Max thought back and remembered the struggles he had with Jay in trying to convince him to leave the bathroom. The difference here was that this child didn't know what he looked like, whereas Jay had. He didn't want to scare her when she did come out. If she came out. He coughed slightly to clear his throat.

"What your name? You alone?" Max asked, as he pressed his ear to the door.

Small shuffling noises could be heard on the other side as if someone was getting closer to the door, and the small voice responded.

"I'm Joan," she sniffled. "I-I left the room that my daddy was in and I k-knew I wasn't supposed to but then these mean guys started chasing me." Halfway through the sentence, she started sobbing. "I r-ran into this c-closet and closed the door and now you're here. Are you sure they're gone?" Joan kept on, speaking rapidly, her sobs seeming to stop as quickly as they started.

Max smiled a bit at the mercurial and fast-talking child. He genuinely did not want to scare her, but knew he had to get her out of the closet and back to wherever her father was.

"Yes, sure, Joan," Max began soothingly. "My name Max. You need to come out, so we find your family. I little funny-looking like other guys, but I won't hurt you, I will help, okay?"

In a surprisingly short amount of time, the closet door opened, and out came a young girl of no more than five, wearing pajamas decorated in penguins. Showing only curiosity and no fear, she looked straight up at Max. He immediately knelt to her level. Joan stared at him a moment longer before throwing her arms around his neck in an embrace, either not caring or not noticing his pale skin and blood-spattered face. Max sat there in shock for a moment before tentatively patting the small girl's back. Wetness filled his eyes at the unexpected show of affection.

Pulling back, Joan looked up and down the hall before pointing down the hallway. "I came from that way," she declared as she started off down the hall with confidence. Max paused before following little Joan, remembering he had left Jay by himself with his meal.

He didn't want to worry the girl, but knew that without his full brain function, Jay could be vulnerable. Making a decision, he stopped Joan before she could continue.

"Joan, I have a...friend. Over here. I need get him before take you back, but need you follow me close, and if I say do something, you do right away. Can you do that?" Max asked.

Joan beamed. "Sure, Max! I like friends!" He smiled at the girl and brought her back towards the lobby. He stopped her for a moment before they went through the doors. Mindful of what Jay was likely still doing, he made a plan. As he looked into the room he noticed that there was a potted tree just outside the doors where it was unlikely Joan would be able to see up the stairs.

"We go through these doors. When we go, need you to hide behind that tree while get my friend. Okay?" he asked. Joan nodded at him and happily skipped through the door with him, ducking down beside the tree and giving him a thumbs up.

Max returned the gesture and continued up the stairs, where he found Jay still sitting on the landing with the corpse. Max smiled when he got closer, realizing the infected boy was in fact sleeping with the corpse across his lap, the body significantly worse for wear at this point. Max shook Jay gently, who woke with a start, growling before realizing it was Max who woke him. The teen gave Max a bloody grin with a small happy moan.

"Come on, Jay-man. Time get up." Max pushed the body off his lap and helped Jay to his feet.

Before they walked away, he looked Jay in the eyes, holding him by his shoulders.

"Jay-Man, I made friend. Want you to meet but need you to listen. Can you do that, buddy?" Jay look at Max and gave him another smile, blood still dripping onto his already filthy shirt. The meal seemed to have improved not only his understanding but also his spirits. Max smiled at him and continued.

"I met little girl name Joan. We need help get back to family. She isn't like us, Jay." He paused for effect, staring into Jay's eyes. "She NOT for eating, okay? She is going to smell like something make you hungry. But we need to help, not hurt, okay?" Jay frowned a bit, trying to comprehend Max's words before smiling and nodding. Max was relatively confident that he understood, and he walked back down the stairs and around the corner to where Joan was still crouched behind the pot.

Jay paused when he saw the small girl, and Max stood on guard, prepared to tackle the boy if he needed to. He watched Jay's expression closely, looking for any signs of aggression, and was pleased that he saw none.

After staring for a moment, Jay gave the girl a bloody and brilliant grin and shambled over to her. Despite the blood, Joan obviously felt the smile was friendly and jumped up to meet him partway.

The two stared at each other for a moment, then Joan smiled and waved. "Hi, Max's friend. I'm Joan. What's your name?" Jay stared at the girl, a bit of bloody drool hanging from the corner of his mouth. He looked over to Max for help.

Max cleared his throat and replied, "This is Jay. He can't talk, but think he is glad to meet you. He going to help us get back to your family."

With the acceptance and exuberance only a child can have, Joan smiled again and wrapped her arms around Jay's middle.

"Thanks, Jay!" Joan exclaimed, totally ignoring the blood that now stained her penguin pajamas. "Can we go find my daddy now, Max?" she asked, turning to him.

"Yup. Let go find him."

"I think I came from that way," she stated, grabbing Jay's hand, walking him down one of the hallways.

Stunned yet again, Max followed the little girl and Jay down the hall. He noted the little skip in her step as she walked beside Jay. It made Max's chest feel tight and he felt grateful for his increased control. After two turns and one set of stairs, Joan told them she thought her room was just down the hall.

They walked up to the door, and Max hesitated for a second before he let her knock. Putting his ear to the door, he couldn't hear anything.

"You sure this one?" he asked Joan.

The little girl nodded at him.

"Yup! One-four-two-zero. My daddy taught me," she responded proudly, pointing at the number on the door.

Max gave her a small smile and looked down at the blood covering his body, realizing her family might not receive two bloody, infected people as well as she had. He pulled her a few doors away and knelt again. Jay stayed perched at the end of the hall, watching with interest.

"Hey, Joan, don't know if your parents want zombie dropping you off, so we going to wait right there behind corner where Jay stand," he said, pointing to his left. "But we stay until you get in, okay?"

Max had really come to like the little girl in the short time he had known her, and he didn't want to cause problems. Joan smiled and hugged him again, squeezing tightly around his neck. This time Max hugged her back. Very subtly he smelled her, and while he could still detect that same enticing scent, he also didn't feel tempted by it, especially coming out of such a small and cute vessel.

"Thanks for saving me, Max. And it was nice to meet you, Jay. You guys are like my bestest friends," she said cheerily as she waved at Jay and skipped back down the hall.

Max positioned himself behind the corner, peeking out, and gave her a thumbs up and a smile. Joan returned the gesture, still holding her thumb up as she knocked on the door.

Before Max or Jay had time to react, the door opened, and Joan screamed as a figure growled and yanked her into the room by her arm. The heavy door slammed shut behind her.

CHAPTER 11

The morning after Clara had spoken to Three and Seventeen, a new person came downstairs, different from the others who watched them.

The first difference Clara noticed was that she was a woman. Secondly, she wore all white, as opposed to the dark greys, blacks, and greens of the others watching them. The third thing she noticed was the curious gleam in her eyes, so different from the aggressive look of most of the people she had encountered so far. Clara watched her, uneasy about anything different than could bring change to the temporary peace of confinement.

The woman walked halfway across the room before turning to one of the soldiers standing behind her.

"Have any of them shown any signs of intelligence or speech?" Rachel asked briskly.

The soldier she had addressed, Private Roberts, looked a bit surprised, but started to shake his head before stopping to consider the question for a moment.

"Actually, there's that grey dude over there. Pretty quiet usually. Always looked to me like he was thinkin' a little harder than some of these undead assholes," he laughed, eliciting a chorus of repeats from the others around them.

With a fake smile, she asked him to point out the one he was talking about.

Clara tensed when she realized they were talking about Three, and struggled to retain her aloof composure, as Three himself had directed her.

What would they do? Clara wondered. *What happened to those others that Three and Seventeen had talked about before?* Panic and awful scenarios ran through Clara's mind, immobilizing her.

The woman in white approached the cage, making several of Clara's roommates go wild trying to reach her. Three sat in his spot in the back like usual, and Clara willed him to get up and act stupid. Three sat there in silence like a petulant teenager, just staring ahead, perfectly aware of what was happening.

"Please bring him upstairs for me," she asked the soldiers, not taking her eyes off Three. She ignored the muttering and objections directed at her as she continued, "But be gentle. If you ask me, you are all entirely too rough," she scolded, turning on her heels and walking through the heavy doors and back up the stairs behind them.

The five men turned back to the cage once the woman had left, and Clara noticed a feral glint in their eyes that was not unlike many of her 'friends' in the cage. Clara instinctually started growling, a light rumble in her throat, her brow furrowed.

One of them immediately took charge as the alpha, advising the rest to pull out their cattle prods and pistols. While Clara didn't know what all of those words meant exactly, she did understand that it wasn't something good, and recognized him as the man from the van who took her. The other caged occupants immediately became more agitated, but moved away from the door once they saw the weapons.

The soldier who had pointed out Three took a set of keys from his belt and unlocked the door, keeping his eyes inside the cage while two others stood closely with their weapons ready.

The door swung open, and for a moment everything in the room was totally still.

One heartbeat.

Two.

Suddenly, it was a blur of movement and buzzing. Several of the zombies who had visible bite marks, the ones that Clara had previously recognized as having little if any memories from before, rushed forward towards the open door. In a flash, two went down, howling as the electric charges rushed through their bodies. The men holding the prods grinned while several more came forward into the cage, ready for any more of the brave and hungry to rush forward. On seeing their two downed companions, the remaining infected became warier, growling and biting towards the soldiers but not wanting to end up like the others.

The alpha soldier, Johnson, stepped in the cage, kicking one of the downed zombies on his way in, eliciting a yelp that made Clara's blood boil. He grinned and stepped forward. The rest of the group cleared a path around him as he approached Three.

"Come on, you stupid ugly fucker," he goaded as he slowly stepped forward. Three continued to sit against the wall, staring straight at his jailor with contempt but not making any move to get up or defend himself.

Another zombie, a woman this time, rushed towards Johnson and was immediately brought down with a prod followed by several punches and kicks. The alpha ignored this while two of his men continued to beat on the now wailing zombie, who was clearly no further threat. Blood poured from the woman's mouth and face, but the soldiers continued. After another moment, there was a loud crack and the wailing stopped. The female ceased moving.

Seventeen growled and made a move to step forward, but Clara grabbed her arm and shook her head slightly.

"That's enough," Johnson said to the soldiers. "You've had your fun. Now grab this asshole and let's go."

No one put up any further fight as they grabbed Three by the arms and pulled him roughly out of the cage, slamming the door behind them. Three put up no resistance, resigned to whatever fate awaited him.

Clara and Seventeen squeezed each other's hands as they watched the soldiers take him up the same staircase Rachel had left through only moments before. The two women stood in silence, wondering if they would ever see Three again.

Rachel sat in what used to be a storeroom, now emptied out other than a few metal racks that were attached to the floor and the two chairs she had specifically brought in. She couldn't risk any of the infected destroying her lab.

Since her examinations which proved that the infected were not in fact dead, as well as determining where the brain damage was centered, she hoped to prove that rehabilitation was in fact possible. Rachel wasn't stupid. She understood that many of the soldiers had a tendency towards violence, and nothing short of hard proof would ever convince them that their zombies were, in fact, sick people with a stable mania that could likely be managed with time and patience.

She felt slightly ill thinking back on the previous experiments she suspected had taken place in the lab in the Seattle. Soldiers and scientists alike had dissected, tortured, and torn apart their specimens. Rachel hadn't been there, but had heard rumors of fire, amputation, and other various forms of dismemberment. Even at the time when she thought they were truly the undead, she couldn't help but be slightly horrified and sincerely hoped the rumors weren't true. Now that she knew otherwise, she was determined to prevent further loss of life. If she could help one of the infected regain some of their former capacity, perhaps they wouldn't be so inclined to shoot first and ask later.

Rachel sighed to herself, wringing her fingers in her sweater while waiting for her first subject, the man who had been pointed out by Private Roberts. She knew that so much of her success, or lack thereof, would dictate many things about the way humanity treated the infected going forward.

She heard footsteps, and something being dragged closer, and stood up. Two soldiers walked in with Three held between them. Although the soldiers both had a good grasp on the infected man's arms, the intensity with which he stared back at Rachel made her shiver.

"Please, come in," she said, trying to compose herself as she pulled out one of the chairs. One of the soldiers frowned looking at it.

"Doctor, we need to lock him down. Captain Wolfe's orders." Rachel reluctantly agreed, and the infected man was handcuffed, one arm on each side of the metal chair. She dismissed the soldiers, turned on her camera, and shut the door. The infected man now had his back to the door, and she couldn't help but stare for a moment, thinking how normal he looked from behind.

His shoulders and back seemed tense. She wondered how many, if any, emotions the infected could still feel. If this was a normal human in front of her, she would guess he was nervous or apprehensive based on body language. Clearing her throat, she sat in the chair across from him and found him staring at her intently, not moving.

"Hello," Rachel said, unsure of where to begin, "My name is Doctor Rachel Samborski." The man stared blankly at her. She looked down at the paper in front of her detailing where he had been found, as well as where he had been taken since.

"I see you were our 'Subject Three' in Seattle. Do you know where that is?"

Again, no response.

Reddening slightly, she continued. "Do you remember your name?"

No reaction.

"I am a doctor. A virologist. I'm not here to hurt you. I brought you here to help."

She went on, noticing that his shoulders did seem to relax ever so slightly at her words. Thinking that maybe he did understand, she pressed on, this time with a bit more confidence.

"My name is Doctor Rachel Samborski. I am recording this on September 16th, 2019, in the military facility site outside of Abbotsford, BC. Subject A, also known as Three, has been brought in to attempt memory stimulation and regeneration." Rachel declared to the camera recording behind them. Turning her attention back to the man in front of her, she attempted a small smile.

"As I said, I am not here to hurt you. I have been doing studies that have shown that people who have been infected, like yourself, have the potential to regain more brain function. To remember." She watched him closely and noted that, while he didn't respond, he did appear to be listening.

Three was listening, of course, but after his previous interactions was wary of non-infected, regardless of what they said.

"Do you…understand me?" she continued.

Three stared at her, not giving anything away. Rachel sighed and pulled out her medical kit. "I need to do some tests, check some things." She paused. "I will not hurt you…so please don't hurt me."

Rachel approached Three, preparing for the physical.

CHAPTER 12

The moments that followed room 1420 opening were a blur for Max. Immediately after Joan had been pulled into the room, Jay had rushed forward to go after her before Max even had a chance to process what happened. Jay banged on the door and howled, trying to help his small friend.

Max rushed over too, but found the door locked. Even his newfound ability to open doors couldn't help without a key, and he didn't know what else to do. Jay continued his assault on the door, oblivious to the futility.

Max fell back against the wall, stunned, rendered motionless by his inability to help Joan. He listened in horror to the screams on the opposite side of the door.

It seemed like forever before the noises stopped, and even longer still before Jay calmed down and came over to him. The feeling he had now, the useless, hopeless feeling, was worse than any other emotion he could remember.

Max thought about Clara and wondered what had happened to her since he left. Although he couldn't remember many specific details, when he closed his eyes he could see her smile, hear her light laugh floating through his mind. He may not have been able to help Joan, but in that moment, he vowed to himself that he would find Clara and save her from this awful and cruel new world.

Wetness burned in his eyes and it took Jay a few moments of prodding Max before the man finally turned his attention back to the teen. Although Jay obviously lacked a lot of his former self, his expression reflected the loss that Max felt. They stared at one another for a few more moments, letting it sink in, before Max finally stood, not even waiting this time to see if Jay was following.

With newfound resolve, Max decided that he would allow no more distractions. He had a mission and a promise he had made that he needed to keep, and nothing else was going to stop him from getting back to Clara. The regret heavy on his shoulders, Max led Jay back towards the front of the building.

They walked into the once bustling streets of Toronto to see chaos around them. Chaos…and silence. Still wary after the recent events, Max put his hand out and stopped Jay before he could step out any farther.

Wrecked cars littered the street, a few of which were nothing more than burnt husks that still smoldered. Windows all over were shattered. Random objects littered the street along with no fewer than a dozen corpses in the immediate vicinity. A rancid smell hung over the entire area even in the open air, a layer of decay over the city. A little way down Max could see a yellow bus, crushed up against a concrete wall with small silhouettes scattered throughout. Images of Joan flashed through his mind, but he shook them off, knowing that he needed to focus if he was going to accomplish what he was setting out to do.

The overcast grey sky set the mood further, oddly dark despite the early hour of the day. In the distance, he could see a couple figures shambling along the road, the pace and body language indicating they were likely infected.

There were several large skyscrapers around him and Max got the impression that any sounds he made would be easily heard by anyone hiding nearby.

Taking one last look around, he saw no movement other than the gentle whispers of several newspapers swaying in the light breeze.

"Come on, Jay-Man," Max said finally, clear but quiet. The boy's eyes sparked slightly for a moment hearing his old nickname, and for a second Max wondered if Jay's memories were coming back, but after a moment of Jay still staring at him with a goofy grin, Max decided to move on. They worked their way out into the street, Max still on high alert and Jay shuffling absentmindedly behind him. Thankfully, Max did have some idea of where to go, and thought back to the days they had spent in the room.

Before Jay had died, Max had asked him questions about where they were. In particular, where they were in relation to the place Jay had said he was from: Vancouver.

After he saw the pictures of Clara, much of the feeling of forgetfulness lifted off his chest. His brain clicked, and while he still couldn't remember a lot of it, he recognized the feeling he associated with thinking of her, seeing her picture. He knew that was love. He had to get back to her.

Drilling Jay as much as was reasonably possible during the sick teen's progression, he had managed to learn a bit more about approximately where he needed to go.

"Listen Daryl—I mean… Max." Jay *stopped for a moment, overcome with coughing.*

"Vancouver is like…pretty far west. That's the general direction." He *nodded towards one of the walls. Max walked to the window and looked at which street that would mean being on when they left.*

"You won't know which way to go, but I can tell you how to follow the sun. The thing in the sky," Jay *went on. "When morning comes, look which way the sun is coming from. Keep the sun at your back until it hits above your head, and then follow it until it goes down again."*

Max was thankful now for that foresight the boy had and looking up and through the grey skies, he could see one area that seemed brighter almost directly above him. He noted the street he had seen from the window and they set off, heading due west.

For the first few hours after leaving the hotel, there were signs of struggle, but very few signs of life. Walking down one street, they had heard a commotion in one of the stores. They moved quickly past it, not daring to go and investigate.

As the sun began to go down, Max realized he would not be able to follow it at nighttime and didn't want to go in the wrong direction, or encounter anything during the night. He signaled for Jay to follow closely and wandered a few blocks over to where the signs of destruction were slightly fewer. Max knew they needed a safe place, a shelter for the night. Remaining quiet and telling Jay to do the same, they crept around several buildings, looking for an access point.

Max looked for a doorknob he would be able to open but that he didn't think others would be able to easily. Happy with himself for thinking of it that way, he soon chose a small shop that appeared to be closed up.

Max opened the door and stepped in with Jay right behind him. It was dark inside, but the waning sun outside provided them with enough light to see around the space. It looked like most of the food and supplies had already been taken, and Max noticed a few brown spots spread out on the ground in front of him.

Taking another step in, he hesitated as Jay started growling behind him. Max frowned, unsure at what was prompting the sudden aggression. He looked around but still couldn't see anything.

Keeping his voice low, he turned to Jay to tell him to calm down. Before he could get more than the first syllable out, several flashes accompanied by loud noises surrounded them.

It only took Max a moment to register the sounds of gunshots and he fell to the ground, dragging Jay down with him, who was now roaring angrily at whoever was shooting at them.

Max tried to see around the cash registers but only got a vague sense of where the shots were coming from behind the empty aisles.

After a moment, the shooting stopped. Max heard voices across the store, frantically saying things he couldn't hear. Taking the opportunity, he pulled Jay up and rushed towards the door they had come through. Shouts and more shooting started raining behind them, but luckily missed as the two crashed back onto the dark streets of Toronto.

Several blocks later, Max finally slowed down. He didn't think they had been followed. He looked over and caught sight of himself and Jay in the glass of a storefront and quickly realized why the people in the grocery store had shot at them. They both looked awful.

Blood and even a few chunks of viscera clung to both of them in various places, and their pale skin seemed to glow in the dim light.

Max approached the reflection slowly, putting his hands up to his face. He really had avoided it as much as possible after that first look, but since regaining his memories he hadn't seen himself. He rubbed a bit at the scruff covering his face and scoffed, not liking how it looked against the pale skin.

Jay trudged behind him, pawing absently at the reflections in front of him, pulling Max out of his reverie. Sighing, Max motioned for Jay to follow and started looking around for a safe place to go.

Keeping to the edge of the road, Max looked for signs of people. Specifically, he was now looking for a business or building that had been ransacked and left open, therefore unlikely to contain any gun-toting uninfected. He was learning from the experiences he had so far.

After another block, they came across what looked to be a small mom-and-pop corner store. The front door was twisted open and even from outside they could see the mess left behind. Garbage and blood was everywhere, with a few missed items floating around in the middle of it all. Grateful for the diminished regard for smell, Max left Jay outside and performed a quick look through. It was bloody and messy but seemed to be blissfully empty.

Looking down at the carnage, Max scanned around. He was looking for something he could identify as edible, but nothing looked familiar and no bodies had been left despite the blood. He pouted a little and continued his search, but other than a closed door hidden at the back, it was deserted.

"Jay, come," he said as he popped his head back outside. Jay obediently followed, sniffing the air a bit on his entry before turning his head towards the back of the store. Jay started to walk towards the door that Max had left shut. Max stepped forward to grab Jay's arm and held him back, and he recognized the familiar scent. Ensuring Jay was properly seated, Max went back over to the door and put his ear to it again. He couldn't hear anything, and The Smell seemed to be faintly all over in the outside world anyways.

Max figured if they were quiet they would be okay to stay for a few hours. He was getting tired and didn't feel like trying to find another place.

With some effort to keep quiet, they managed to get one of the racks to hold the door shut and both settled behind the till.

Jay quickly fell asleep, snoring deeply into his chest and twitching periodically. Max sat and contemplated all that had happened since leaving the room. It had only been a day, but they had experienced a lot, and the multiple run-ins with both infected and uninfected gave him a lot to think about.

After a while, he reached into his pocket, pulling out the treasured picture of him and Clara. Smiling to himself, he finally drifted off to sleep, thinking of her.

CHAPTER 13

Clara and Seventeen stayed huddled together in one corner of the cage for the hours that followed Three being taken. The soldiers had not removed the body of the female they beat to death, and despite their hunger it took quite a while before one of the others got the confidence to approach. One of the males in the group, who had been one of the bite victims from the van, began nibbling on her first. Once he started it didn't take long for the majority to join him. Now only some scraps and clothes remained.

Although Clara was hungry, she had already figured out that The Smell that made her feel ravenous and anxious wasn't coming from her fellow infected. As her memories came back it seemed her control over her emotions did as well, unlike when she had first attacked the soldiers who took her.

Home.

She thought of the picture in her pocket and wondered if she would ever find that man. Despite her desire to see him, she also hoped he never showed up here. She wouldn't wish this place upon anyone.

Clara looked at the blood-stained floor as she clung to Seventeen, her stomach grumbling in spite of herself. She wondered if their captors were ever going to feed them or if she too would be eating her cellmates before long.

This train of thought had her thinking about Three again, wondering what was happening to him. Just as she started thinking about him, the heavy doors opened and two soldiers entered the room with Three between them.

Clara and Seventeen did their best not to react but both stiffened as they watched the trio make their way across the room. They couldn't see any visible marks on him; however, the grim look on Three's face was anything but encouraging.

The two soldiers threw him back in the cell and placed two buckets near the entrance of the door before slamming it shut behind them.

The occupants all hugged the walls, eyeing the buckets with unease, wary after the soldiers' last visit into the cage. Brushing off invisible lint, Three briefly looked into the buckets before working his way across the room and going to his trademark spot on the back wall. He sat down and put his arms around his knees, acting like nothing had happened.

A faint smell made its way to Clara and curiosity got the better of her. She indicated to Seventeen to stay put while she made her way to the buckets to see what the soldiers had left them. She did not look at Three, sure she would see his disapproval of her actions.

As she approached, she saw one was filled with water and the other some kind of raw meat. Although hesitant to touch anything provided by her captors, Clara's needs beat out her caution and she thirstily gulped water from her hands as her fellow captives watched on with interest.

A moment later, Seventeen came up behind her with the rest following closely behind. While the rest clamored around the water, having mostly gotten their fill of meat earlier, Clara dug into the second bucket and scooped out two large handfuls of the ground meat before making her way over to Three.

Sitting down beside him, she offered one of her handfuls. After a beat, Three accepted, nodding at Clara in thanks as they partook in their respective meals.

Clara moaned in pleasure as she took her first bites, having not eaten since before she turned. Deep in the back of her mind, she wondered if she should have a problem with raw meat, but her hunger quickly stifled those thoughts as she dove into the rest.

Sitting back finally sated and content, Clara leaned her head forward to look over at Three again, who was still absently nibbling his handful while looking straight ahead. Concern crossed her face and she reached out to touch his arm.

Stiffening at her touch, Three brought the meat down from his face and looked back at Clara. After a moment, he put his head downwards and just barely whispered the word, "Later."

Understanding this wasn't the time to ask questions, Clara grabbed Three's empty hand and waited and watched while Seventeen divvied out the rest of the buckets.

While the zombies ate their fill, Rachel was sitting upstairs, thinking about her recent interview.

Rachel had sat with Three for almost two hours, just talking to him about anything and everything while inspecting his body. While he hadn't prevented her from doing so, he didn't make it easy or respond to any of her questions.

The entire time she spoke, Rachel had very much gotten the sense that he was listening. While Three tried not to react, his general attention and awareness was a giveaway compared to his relatively mindless counterparts.

Stirring a cup of weak instant coffee, Rachel pored over the files and notes that had been compiled on the almost two dozen infected they had downstairs. Out of all of them, fifteen had bite marks and injuries on various parts of their bodies, which indicated to her that they had turned from a direct bite as opposed to having caught the virus organically.

Sipping the hot drink absently, Rachel thought back to Seattle, where one of the soldiers who stood guard for their original group had been bitten.

By that point of the virus's progression, virologists were relatively sure that those who hadn't yet caught the disease were immune. Exposure was almost inevitable, and many of the people who remained uninfected had encountered the virus in one way or another and remained healthy. While scientists studied the data of those who had not contracted the virus, Rachel was the first to witness a person previously thought to be immune turn after a vicious bite.

The soldier had teased the occupants with the buckets' contents for hours before entering to place them down, and when he did, he was less than careful. One daring and hungry infected rushed forward, biting the young soldier on his forearm.

The infection from the bite spread hard and fast, and in under two days he died, as opposed to those who contracted the virus where it typically took 5-7 days. Less than ten minutes after calling time of death, the soldier had gotten up again and ripped the throat out of the attending nurse, who bled out quickly while nearby guards took out their infected companion. The nurse was quickly removed as well.

Rachel thought about that now and wondered if there was any difference of brain damage between those who were bitten and those who were not. Looking at the profile of the one infected she had done CT and MRI scans on in Seattle, she noticed that he was one of those bitten.

She decided it was time to do some tests and imaging on one who had died from the virus as opposed to a bite. Looking over the few who had apparently died from the virus itself, Rachel selected one of the females who appeared relatively healthy, one of their newer arrivals, and scheduled her to be brought up for a round of scans.

Getting up, she poured out her coffee and left to find Captain Wolfe and let him know what she needed.

Of course, Rachel had no way of knowing she had just selected Clara, and that her choice would change both of their lives forever.

CHAPTER 14

The next day, the sky seemed to open up as water poured down steadily from the foreboding clouds. Looking upwards, Max couldn't see any sign of the sun to guide them, and they hadn't had enough time to go over maps in order for him to find his way otherwise. As much as he wanted to get moving, he didn't want to go the wrong way and have to backtrack.

"Pass me some of the books from over there," Jay asked Max, pointing at the desk in the corner with the glossy hotel and tourist brochures. Bringing them over to Jay, Max sat on the edge of the bed. Opening one of the books, Jay found an enlarged map of Canada and pointed to Toronto.

"This is a map of Canada. I don't know where to find a map you can use, but the sun should work out for this time of year," Jay began pointing to the city in the book in front of him.

"This is Vancouver way over here by the water. It's like…Over 4000 kilometers away." Jay thought for a second. He was actually very good at math in school, and quickly tried to average out the distance in his head.

"If you walk, like…the whole way, it would take you way over a month to do." Jay concluded, frowning, not totally sure how Max would ever be able to do such a thing.

Max contemplated Jay's word for a moment before asking, "So a day means sun up and down right? So…lots of those until at Clara?" to which Jay nodded, hoping his slow friend understood the distance involved at least a little bit.

Pausing again, Jay considered the problem.

"Maybe you can find another way? A car, or…." Before Jay could finish, he was retching over the side of the bed again.

They didn't get a chance to talk about it further.

Max took a moment to consider the conversation that occurred before Jay died. He had been thinking about it the night before and realized the journey was going to be more difficult that he originally thought. He knew it really would be a good idea for them to find another way to Vancouver. Walking was going to take too long, especially if they kept having to stop.

Unfortunately, he didn't know how to read a map, much less operate a car. He looked to Jay, saddened that there was still no improvement in the boy's recovery. Max couldn't help but wonder what other ideas he may have had, but accepted that he would likely never know.

Making a decision, he turned to Jay, who was still leaning against the counter staring at the raindrops running down one of the jagged windows.

"Jay, we stay here for now. Rain stop soon, then we go," Max stated, crouching down and still keeping his voice low. Jay grinned back at him in apparent understanding and resumed his vigilant watch of the water droplets. Max stood by the door, watching rain fill the streets.

At least it's washing some of the blood away, Max thought to himself as he stared glumly at the downpour that was keeping him from Clara. Looking down at his own filth-covered body, including what was once a white dress shirt now multicolored with gore, he got an idea.

"Jay, come here," Max commanded gently as he put out his hand for the boy.

Uncertain of Max's intention, Jay hesitated slightly before grasping his hand.

He instructed Jay to help him push the rack blocking the door out of the way. He cringed at the screech of metal and completed the task as quickly as possible before stepping out into the downpour.

Lifting his face to the sky, Max extended his arms and let the rain wash over him. Seeing the joy in his face, Jay quickly joined him. As he stepped out, Jay seemed to decide that he liked the feeling of the rain hitting his body and began doing a strange sort of disjointed prance around Max, a strange guttural laugh escaping his lips. Max laughed at the silliness and happiness he was seeing in Jay and joined him in celebrating the rain.

The last twenty-four hours had been stressful and the awkward happy dance combined with the rain lightened both of their hearts. Together they ran in circles until they were both soaked, but considerably cleaner and happier.

After about an hour of this, the rain hadn't let up, and Max led them back inside. His stomach suddenly growled loudly, making Jay giggle and surprising Max. He realized how hungry he was and started looking around for something to eat.

A few random chocolate bars and bags of chips were among the debris but held no interest to Max. He figured he could probably figure out how to open them but remembered that that was what Jay had been eating before he turned, and it hadn't smelled particularly appetizing then.

Sniffing the air, Max caught a faint whiff of the ever elusive and delicious

Smell. *Oh yeah, the other door!* he thought. He realized they hadn't heard any noises through the night and put his ear against it to listen. He debated for a few moments, thinking of the guns that greeted them behind the last closed door, but when he considered that there was probably fresh, delicious meat on the other side of that door, his hunger won out.

I won't even have to feel bad for hurting someone, Max preened to himself. *I can be full and not feel guilty!*

Telling Jay to stay back, he opened the door as quietly as he could.

Peering into the gloomy interior, he stopped and listened again for a moment. Satisfied that he wouldn't immediately get shot, Max opened it the rest of the way. A stronger, more immediate smell wafted towards them, causing Jay to stand at attention. Waving him down to stay quiet, Max moved forward and realized this was some kind of living area behind the store. Aged brown walls and taupe carpet covered the hall. The lack of light made it seem particularly gloomy. Several pictures lined the walls beside him, but it was too dark to see clearly, and he was focused on what was ahead. The rain pattered on, the only noise immediately noticeable.

To Max's right was what he recognized as a kitchen, with some kind of den down the hall in front of them.

Max stopped in front of the kitchen entrance lifting his nose to the air. *No fresh blood scent here, but maybe they have meat. Kitchens have meat and food,* he rationalized, and he stepped into the small space. Following closely behind, Jay suddenly moaned and turned and quickly began shuffling further down the hall towards the den.

Cursing internally, Max quickly followed after him as they both stepped into the den.

"Stop! Stay here," Max whispered to Jay angrily, indicating a chair in front of them. Lowering his head in shame, Jay sat down and whimpered slightly but was otherwise still.

Max decided checking the rest of the apartment was a good idea anyways and looked to Jay to ensure he stayed in place. The place seemed as gloomy as the hallway; however, it didn't have any of the wreckage that the front of the building did. Max vaguely wondered where the owners were.

As he walked towards what looked to be a hallway of more rooms, the fine hairs on the back of his neck stood up. Something felt very off, and his fear of guns and people made him slow his pace as he moved forward. Sensing Max tense, Jay sat up in his chair and moaned lightly, but stayed where he was in deference to Max's earlier display of dominance.

Max heard the tiniest noise that almost reminded him of Joan. He stopped and looked around for a moment before registering where the noise had come from. Max looked to his side, and sure enough, several sets of eyes stared back at him from a crack in the adjacent closet. They all widened at the same time as Max panicked. "We not hurt you!" he exclaimed to the fearful eyes.

At Max's words the eyes seemed to widen even further, and he heard a small voice. "Mommy, did that zombie just talk?" Another small voice started crying and he heard a woman's voice shush in response.

Holy shit, he thought, *there's a whole family in there! They must have been hiding since they heard us banging on the door outside.* Max immediately stepped back into the den. Jay stood at the ready, curious but oddly no longer showing signs of aggression.

Max put a hand on Jay's chest to indicate he stay still. Max's stance was tense and ready to bolt at the slightest threat. However, he figured if the people in the closet had a gun, they probably would have used it already. He thought about leaving but didn't want to go back out in the rain or have to find another place to hide.

"We are zombie," Max said as clearly as he could, "but we not hurt you." The crying slowed a bit and he heard frantic whispers.

"We hide from rain," Max continued, hoping to calm them with his words. "Were looking for food."

Shit, he thought. *Did I just say that to the people that are afraid of me?*

"Not people food! Other type food...." He trailed off, unsure of how to salvage that one.

Before he could continue, the door creaked open and a small Asian woman emerged with a bat in hand. She watched Max closely as she closed the door behind her.

For several moments they just stared at one another until a small girl's voice whispered for her mother. At hearing this, Jay tried to move forward, causing the woman to swing the bat in his direction. Her expression was one of determination, despite the tears running down her face.

Max turned around and frowned at Jay. "What doing, Jay? Stop scaring them." Jay immediately stopped trying to move forward, but his expression dropped, and he looked sad. Jay opened his mouth as if to say something. "Joooa...."

Max stared at his friend, absolutely stunned for a moment. Jay had finally tried to talk! And it almost sounded like he said...

Suddenly, Max realized why Jay was so eager to get towards the closet. Turning to the woman, he put his palms facing outward to address her once more.

"He not hurt you. He hear voice of girl...sound like our friend.... Sound like Joan," Max said sadly, looking back at Jay.

"Joan gone now. Jay just wanted say hi. This Jay, I am Max."

The bat lowered slowly throughout Max's speech as the woman's expression went through a range of emotions in seconds, ending somewhere near bewilderment.

"I—I have never heard a zombie speak," the woman finally responded, only a slight accent in her voice.

Max smiled sadly at this and replied as honestly as he could. "We not all speak."

She considered this for a moment, the bat lowered, but still firmly in her grasp. Making a decision, she turned back to the closet and opened it, whispering inside. A moment later, two children emerged: a boy of about eight and girl just a bit younger. They stood behind their mother, watching them curiously. Max did his best to smile reassuringly and the slight moan behind him told him Jay was giving his own brand of silly grin.

"I am Sue. This is Lucy and…"

"I'm Charlie, but my friends call me Chip!" the little boy interrupted as he stepped out and smiled at Max. Chip turned to his mother and smiled. "Mom, this is *so* cool!"

CHAPTER 15

Clara was asleep at the back of the cage leaning on Three's shoulder when the gates opened again. She wasn't completely awake, but suddenly heard Three begin to growl and was pushed aside as he stood up. Looking up, she saw the soldiers coming towards them, their eyes focused on her.

Clara's eyes widened as she realized they weren't here for Three this time. He continued to growl, and she remembered the female who had fought back before, the scraps of clothing still on the ground a grim reminder. Clara knew that he wouldn't put up a fight for himself, but for her he might. Not wanting Three to get himself killed for her, she stepped in front of him and looked into his eyes, hoping he would read her intent, before turning to the soldiers. She glared at them but stood her ground.

One of the men, Private Brody, watched this exchange with interest before pushing forward and grabbing Clara's arm.

More gently than she anticipated, she was led out of the cage and through the door which filled her with such dread.

A few moments later she was handcuffed and placed in a chair in a small room before the door closed and she was left alone. Using the slack between the cuffs, she placed her hand on the edge of her pocket. Even her fingers proximity to the photo that lay inside giving her reassurance. Before Clara could get comfortable, the door opened, making her head shoot up and her heart race.

Rachel closed the door and looked over at Clara. Noticing she looked apprehensive, Rachel put a small smile on her face and tried to use slow movements to get over to the chair across from Clara.

"My name is Rachel Samborski," she began as she looked Clara up and down to make sure no recent visible bites had occurred while in captivity.

"I am not going to hurt you. I just want to talk," she continued.

Clara eyed the doctor warily, understanding her words but not believing them. She thought back to all of her interactions with humans since she woke up. Being taken from her home, waking up confined with a bag on her head, the cage, the stories from Three and Seventeen, the female beaten to death by the soldiers.... At this last memory, she began growling at Rachel, who paled considerably but, to her credit, didn't flinch.

Clearing her throat, Rachel did her best to ignore the angry look she was receiving and pressed onwards. *At least this zombie isn't jumping around trying to bite me like some of them*, she observed.

"I am not going to hurt you," Rachel repeated. "I am a doctor, not a soldier. And I am doing studies on people like yourself. People who were infected with the FIRE virus. Do you know what that is?"

Clara stared at her, the growl in her throat mellowing as she listened.

"We believe people like yourself could have the ability to get better. To remember."

At this last part, Clara visibly perked up a bit, thinking of the picture in her pocket and what she would give to remember the man. Rachel noticed the spark in Clara's eyes and continued, encouraged by the subtle, but real, response.

"I can help you remember things, I believe. If you can understand me, can you nod your head?" Rachel asked hopefully.

Clara considered this for a moment but remembered too well the warning from Three and Seventeen about the smarter ones. She was already worried that she had given herself away with the meat bucket and decided to stay silent.

Rachel sighed as she considered what to do next. *I suppose I should do the blood work then scans next*, she thought to herself. *I can do the physical and use that data, anyways.* Getting up slowly, she started to approach Clara, who visibly tensed in her seat.

Keeping her voice even and calm, she tried to explain. "It is okay. I need to do a few tests. You just need to stay still for me. Can you do that?" Rachel said as soothingly as she could manage.

"Our tests show that your pain receptors likely aren't working very well. You shouldn't feel anything, but there will be needles." Rachel pulled out her medical bag and put it on her chair as she looked at Clara. Studying the infected woman for a minute, she tried to take her features in on a scientific level.

Well, her skin is quite pale even for a Caucasian woman, Rachel thought. *Iris appears to be very pale as is also indicative of the infected, although this one seems to be particularly so, which could indicate she had blue eyes prior.* Rachel noticed the gold ring still on her left ring finger and wondered where her partner was.

Clara gazed back at Rachel, a little confused by the looks she was getting. Shaking her head out of her musings, Rachel pulled some syringes out of her bag.

"I just need to draw some blood. Like I already said, it shouldn't hurt, but just...growl if you want me to stop, okay?" Rachel sputtered, realizing how silly that sounded. Even still, she got no resistance when she uncuffed one of her arms and put the band around Clara's arm to begin filling vials. Clara stared at her face, not caring about what was happening with the needle in her arm.

Who is this doctor? Clara wondered as her blood filled the tubes.

A few minutes later she was finished, and Rachel turned her back to Clara, taking a few moments to prepare and pack away the vials. Clara realized that this small act of turning her back in itself showed a huge degree of trust. Either that, or ignorance. Clara had seen how her lesser companions drooled and fought over the smell of living flesh. Even now, she felt the urge. The only difference was that her memories provided her a degree of control. If she wanted to badly enough, she could easily tear this woman's throat out right now. A moment later, she was interrupted from her thoughts as the doctor turned back around to address her.

"Okay, now I just need to take you to another room to scan your head. I don't want to hurt you," Rachel repeated again, leaning down to unlock the second cuff. "If you would please, come with me."

Clara stared at the woman intently. While she wasn't quite ready to talk to her, she wouldn't fight back either. She willingly let the doctor take her by the arm.

Rachel helped Clara stand and knocked on the door, indicating for the soldier on the other side to open it.

Clara flinched slightly at the sight of the men, but continued on beside Rachel, who held her head high, barely even acknowledging their presence. Together they walked down the stark hallways until they arrived at a lab. Rachel quickly informed the guards to stay outside and pulled Clara into the room.

Looking around the room, Clara saw all kinds of things she didn't think she would have been able to identify even before she died. The entire room smelled funny even to Clara's reduced sense of smell. Silver, white, and glass were everywhere she looked, and some small part of her enjoyed the order of it. Even the refrigerator looked high tech and complicated. Her eyes dazzled at the cleanliness.

Rachel stood and watched Clara's gaze as she looked around the room and recognized it as something close to awe.

"Pretty great, isn't it?" Rachel smirked, causing Clara to quickly school her features. "Come on, the scans are in these rooms over here."

Without looking to see if she was followed, Rachel moved through the room with familiarity towards a door in the left corner.

"I need to scan you, like I said already," Rachel began, an idea forming in her mind as she prepared the first few slides. "Let me prep a few tests before, though. Why don't you take a seat."Without thinking, Clara looked around and found the nearest stool and pulled it out, sitting down on the high metal chair. She looked up to see Rachel staring at her with wide eyes before she realized what she'd done.

"You understood me!" Rachel gasped.

Clara became frantic. *What the hell will they do to me now?* Her instincts kicked in and she went from panic to defense as she snarled, standing and preparing to defend herself.

Rachel caught herself taking a step back before deciding to hold her ground. She was beginning to realize that this infected woman, and probably the other man, Number Three from the other lab, both had been playing dumb. There had been a few times she felt certain they understood, and the focus was there. Rachel had suspected before but had just confirmed that something…some*one* that was considered a braindead zombie actually understood her and could listen and respond to instructions. *I was right!*

For a moment, the women stared at each other, Clara trying to ascertain the threat level while Rachel's brain raced and tried to figure out why they would pretend they couldn't understand.

Suddenly she remembered the uncomfortable reaction to the soldiers before and thought back to the experiments. Rachel wondered what else the soldiers did that she didn't know about. Did this woman in front of her somehow know about the experiments that went on prior to her arrival?

"I won't tell the others," Rachel spat out quickly, hoping she was correct in her assumptions and that she wasn't about to get eaten by a zombie in her own lab.

After a moment Clara stopped growling but didn't sit again, continuing to stare at Rachel warily.

Quickly taking her opportunity, Rachel did her best to pretend it hadn't happened and carefully led Clara to the MRI chamber.

Rachel decided to continue the rest of her tests, knowing she had a bit of a wait ahead of her while the scans did their thing. Most of them were pretty standard—checking the basic body chemistry, hormone levels, and other rather mundane things.

She printed out and processed the results over thirty minutes while the scan completed, noting which tests she would need to come check on hours later. She flipped through them absently and what she considered to be her "science brain" took over as she scanned through the results while turning off the machine. She turned on the microphone and told Clara she could get out. Heading towards the door, she finished the page, about to put the printouts down to finish reading later.

Stopping in her tracks, she turned around and looked at the screen again, confirming what she had just read.

Holy shit, Rachel thought to herself as she looked at the data. Over the microphone with a shaky voice she told Clara to hold tight for a few minutes, needing a moment to process. She wasn't overly surprised when the woman seemed to comply and sit on the edge of the MRI machine eyeing the door with mild unease.

Turning back to her computer, Rachel stared at it for a few moments, letting her mind catch up with it.

This woman's HGC levels were through the roof. *She is pregnant!*

Clara sat in the MRI chamber, wondering what was happening. Was this when they would come in and take her and torture her? Worried, she found herself touching the picture in her pocket again for reassurance. If that happened, she would never find out who the man was. Her eyes burned with tears she didn't know how to shed as she thought of him. It was like the memory of his face was imprinted on her soul in such a way to make her feel comforted with his image alone.

After a few minutes the door opened and Rachel walked back in; Clara immediately noticed the strange expression on her face. She wasn't looking at Clara like a zombie or a threat. In fact, she was looking at her like she would another uninfected human. And she looked worried.

Clearing her throat, she looked Clara in the eyes.

"I know you can understand me," Rachel started. "I know you are afraid, but I won't tell them. I am a scientist. A doctor. I want to help you, and others like you." She filled her voice with as much sincerity as possible, and despite herself Clara found that she believed it.

"I don't know if you can talk already, but I think you will be able to. I can maybe help you with that later, but for now, can you please, *please* nod or say something if you understand me?" Rachel pleaded.

For several minutes neither of them moved, a standoff-style staring contest. Although she knew it might be the wrong choice, Clara gave the slightest of nods to indicate she understood, not wanting to give away her speaking ability quite yet. At this, Rachel sighed as her whole body seemed to deflate.

"I knew it," Rachel gloated excitedly. "I *totally* told them so!" Without thinking about it, she did a tiny jig right there in the MRI room, much to Clara's astonishment.

Looking up, Rachel barked out a small laugh at Clara's expression before stifling it and pulling herself together. With a lot more seriousness, she looked Clara in the eyes. "We really need to talk."

Clara looked at her with apprehension and interest.

Sighing again, she spit it out.

"I was running some tests while you were in there. I don't know who you were before…I mean…before you died…you were pregnant. You still are, even though you died, otherwise the levels of HGC would have dropped by now," Rachel attempted to explain, not realizing that after the word 'pregnant' Clara had stopped listening.

Even with her slower brain, this word immediately resonated with Clara and brought back an immediate rush of emotions and memories. *Pregnant. Home.* Her eyes widened and without thinking about it, one word slipped out of her mouth.

"Max."

CHAPTER 16

After a small bump where Sue hit Jay with a bat when she thought he was going to bite Lucy, they all managed to settle in relatively well. For the first few hours, Sue watched them both with unease, but surprised even herself at her own comfort level with the two zombies who now occupied her home. She was a person who prided herself on her instincts, and despite her first reaction of terror, her gut felt as though she could trust them. She even pulled out a few steaks that were nearly frozen for the two of them, much to Max's delight.

Lucy and Chip were immediately attracted to Jay and his silly, brainless demeanor. He smiled at the children, let them show him toys, poke him and just laugh at his confused expressions. Every time they laughed, Jay would grin and his eyes would light up. While Sue still seemed on edge, she loved seeing her children smile and laugh for the first time since they had holed away in their home.

While Jay and the children played, Max decided to ask Sue some questions.

"Sue…maybe help me?" he asked her. Surprised that a zombie would need her help, she agreed to help if she was able.

"Max and Jay go to Vancouver."

"Vancouver!" Sue exclaimed. "That is on the other side of the country! Why are you going there?"

Max pulled out his wallet, showing her the picture of him and Clara.

"I go to Clara."

Sue held out her hand and Max handed her the wallet. She held it in her lap and stared at it for a few minutes before handing it back. When she looked up, tears lined her eyes.

"You are trying to find your wife," she said, simply. Max nodded.

She was his Clara, not his wife. But he understood what Sue was trying to say. Still, he didn't understand the tears in her eyes and pointed at them by way of question.

Sue chuckled in response, wiping the stray tear from the corner of her eye.

"I was always a sucker for a love story. Never thought I'd cry at a zombie romance, though."

Standing up, she walked back through the house and returned a moment later with a photo of her own. Handing it to Max, she sat down again, this time beside him.

"This was my husband. He died two years ago, before all of this." Max stared at the photo of the family in his hands. Both Lucy and Chip were considerably smaller, he noticed. And Sue looked much...brighter.

Thinking of Clara, he felt bright too. Max handed the photo back and smiled at Sue.

"Sue does understand! Max and Jay go find Clara."

"Yes, I understand, Max." Sue smiled before her face dropped slightly. "I do understand, Max, but it's just me and the kids. I can't leave to help you. But if there is another way I can help, I will. We have time before the rain stops. Let me think for a while, okay?" Taking the picture back, she did what no other mother had ever done before her: she left her children to play with some zombies while she tried to figure out how to get them across the country.

"Can you do this, Jay?" Chip chirped, as he stuck his tongue out and touched his nose.

Jay watched the boy intently before sticking his tongue out. "Blehhh." He tried, his tongue staying flat.

Chip seemed to find this hilarious, while Lucy ignored them both as she painted Jay's nails a particularly vivid shade of pink. Jay didn't seem to mind and in fact seemed to enjoy the small girl fussing over him.

Standing over them, Max watched the interactions and found himself glad that Jay was able to not only handle, but excel at, being around children, despite the smell he knew must be tempting him.

It had been almost a week since Jay had turned and he still hadn't really improved insofar as his ability to speak, although he obviously understood to a reasonable degree. Max wondered if he was just a fluke since all the other infected he had encountered so far had been more like Jay than himself. None had spoken like him. As his mind wandered down this path it stumbled upon Clara, and he wondered what he would find when he returned home. *Will she be like me?*

CHAPTER 17

Rachel had been in virology for almost ten years. She was an incredibly logical person, and despite having gone through medical school, she went the route of a researcher instead of a practitioner. The moral and ethical dilemmas that came with dealing with people were something she simply didn't care to deal with; viruses didn't discriminate. They were straightforward and easy to understand.

Although she had already altered the records to keep this secret for now, she didn't know what to do with the information. To turn Clara over to Wolfe or his men was paramount to killing her and her baby.

Oh god, she thought to herself. *I am talking about trying to save a zombie baby, for chrissakes!*

Even though Rachel had suspected they had the ability to speak, hearing a name come from this infected woman's lips still surprised her.

Before Rachel could react to hearing the name, Clara pulled something out of her robe pocket and brought it to her lap.

Immediately Rachel leaned over and was shocked even further to see what she held.

It was a photo. Even more importantly, it was of the woman in front of her, obviously some time before she turned.

"Is that Max?" Rachel asked softly.

For a second, Clara didn't respond.

Until a moment before, she hadn't remembered his name. The memories of him, of them together, raced through her mind. A small part of her felt guilt that she had forgotten him, but she quickly pushed that out of her mind.

"Yes." Clara finally replied simply.

Unsure of what else to say, Rachel waited.

"This Max. Home." She handed the photo over to Rachel, who took it despite the bits of dirt and god knows what else on it. Looking up at Rachel for clarification, she asked a

simple question.

"Baby?"

Rachel looked at the photo a moment longer before handing it back to Clara. "Yes. Inside you there is a baby."

Clara intuitively picked up the words that hadn't been said and asked another question. "Men…Bad men take baby?" She held her hand over her stomach protectively.

"I won't tell them but…. I'm sorry, I just don't know…."

After confirming the records of the pregnancy were all completely eradicated and modified to reflect what she thought appropriate, she had gone to speak with Wolfe, one on one, about the report she had made earlier in the week. While she couldn't use her most recent findings, she hoped to improve the treatment of the infected while she made a plan for Clara.

"What do you mean you knew they could speak!" Rachel shouted at Captain Wolfe, her voice shrill, even to her own ears. He sat across the desk from her with a look that told her he would rather be anywhere but there talking to her.

He leaned forward, tightening his eyes.

"In Seattle, there were a number of zombies who showed heightened intelligence. It makes no difference though, as they all still attacked *my* men," he responded. "I do NOT give a shit how smart they are or not."

"Then why have you been letting me study them this whole time?"

"Because it keeps you busy and not bothering me. Like now."

"Who attacked first, Captain?" Rachel spat tersely. "Did even one of them attack your men first or did you ever consider they were responding the way any person would, by defending themselves?" At this, Wolfe laughed freely.

"People?" he said, still laughing. "They are fucking zombies!" he finished, shouting as he stood up.

"Listen, Dr. Samborski. And listen closely," Wolfe continued, standing over her. "You are only here for show. Your teams, your research, none of it matters anymore. There won't be a cure. No magic solution. My job is to keep us safe and kill anyone who stands in the way of *civilized*, healthy people."

Rachel immediately understood the implied threat and her eyes narrowed. Wolfe walked back around to his desk and sat down.

"I suggest you decide quickly which side you are on," he continued, watching her closely for a reaction.

"Smith," he yelled to a soldier standing outside the room, "escort Doctor Samborski back to her lab."

Rather than return to her lab, where she knew her co-workers would be back by now, Rachel decided to go to her bunk. As one of the few women who wasn't a soldier, she was afforded the luxury of a private area. It seemed to her like she had been sleeping in her lab mostly anyways, but in times like this she was grateful for the privacy.

The revelations of the past few hours whirled through her head as she started to formulate a plan. It wasn't a good plan, but it seemed like there would be no such thing in the world of FIRE.

CHAPTER 18

Sue came back to the den and smiled as she watched her children encourage Jay to make funny faces. There was so little to laugh at these days, even before the virus hit.

After her husband's death, Sue had been left with a small business and two children under ten. As an immigrant, a business owner, a mother, and now a widow, life had not been easy. Despite the odds stacked against her, she had somehow come out of it on top. Her children were well adjusted, smart, and well fed. The shop, while not thriving, supported them well enough, even in one of the most expensive cities in the country. Something had been missing for a long time though, and coming out of her bedroom she realized what it was.

Laughter. Joy.

While they had gotten by, the children hadn't truly been carefree in years and she knew that a large part of that was due to her playing the role of both parents. Sue knew that performing both roles meant she needed to be twice as hard, twice as disciplined. Seeing Chip and Lucy giggling with Jay, as Max looked over them all with a fond look on his face, she felt something she hadn't in a long time. A sense of family.

Clearing her throat, she made the room aware of her entrance. Both Chip and Lucy immediately turned towards their mother, but Jay took a moment longer, stuck mid-silly face. By his unsurprised face and posture, Sue guessed Max had already been aware of her presence.

"I think maybe it's time for dinner," Sue announced before flushing deeply and realizing she was about to face another circumstance a mother likely hadn't prior to this day. She was offering to feed two zombies dinner.

As though reading her train of thought, Max smiled kindly at her.

"I help make. Jay watch kids." He looked down at the trio, goofing around on the floor together. "Well, they watch each other at least."

Sue nodded in agreement and together they walked towards the kitchen, both lost in their own thoughts on how to navigate this next chapter.

Before entering the familiar space, she walked over to the door leading to the front of the store and put her ear towards it. After a moment, she nodded to herself and walked back to the kitchen. Max watched this with interest before finally asking a question that had been plaguing him for awhile.

"What happen out there? Not in here?" He pointed at the door. While there were some words missing, Max was quite good by now at making his intent known, and Sue understood the question he was trying to ask. What had happened and how they had stayed safe and undetected back here.

Taking advantage of the distraction, Sue filled a pot with water and placed it on top of a small kerosene burner that had been set on the counter. She gathered her thoughts for a moment and started her story.

"When the news reports came out, I pulled the children from school right away. Where we come from, Japan, there are lots of people, and disease spreads fast, so I suppose it was a carryover of my own upbringing."

Max nodded in understanding and interrupted briefly, pointing at what she was doing. "I help?"

Sue shook her head as she continued. "A few days later when the reports said the virus had hit New York, I closed the store and moved the most important things, like non-perishable food, back here. There is an old crawlspace in the bedroom; I hid most of the food back there that didn't need to be kept cold. We stayed quiet and listened to the broadcasts, just waiting for news. Honestly, the waiting was the worst part. The electricity went out and has flickered on and off a few times. When we heard the front door crash open, we all hid in the crawlspace. There was an awful commotion. We could hear it even from back there. The door lock has been broken for a long time and I remember kicking myself for not fixing it sooner. No one ever came into the house, but when the noises stopped I still waited."

She poured some noodles into the now boiling water.

"Lucy was terrified. It took a long time to get her to calm down. Finally, I left them hiding and came out to check by myself." She smiled to herself. "Chip was so brave. Told me he would look after Lucy and take good care of her even though I told them I would only be a few minutes. He is such a good boy…."

Getting back on her train of thought, she continued. "The store was a mess, but we were safe. When you came it was a few days later, and we heard the noises again we hid until we thought you were gone, but when the door opened to the apartment we didn't have time to get to the crawlspace. We hid in the closet and, well…you know the rest." Sue smiled warily at him as she tried to think of how to ask her next question.

"Max, I am making the children pasta. The steaks I pulled out earlier should be almost thawed. I can't help but wonder, though, what else can you eat? Other than the obvious, of course." A small twinkle in her eyes gave away the attempt at humor and Max smiled mirthlessly even though his mind was overridden with guilt.

This poor family shouldn't have to worry about feeding us, he thought to himself. His stomach, however, disagreed and growled loudly, causing Sue to giggle. The tension was broken.

Max thought about her question for a moment, not quite sure how to answer. He knew that people smelled good, but he had also eaten food that he had found in the hotel room after he first turned, though he couldn't remember what it was anymore. Max did remember that it hadn't been very satisfying and couldn't recall smelling anything that tempted him as much as human flesh. He hadn't really been exposed to much else, other than the junk food Jay had tried to eat before he died.

Deciding to find out more, for his own benefit as well as Jay's, he leaned across the kitchen towards the place Sue had left the steaks out and inhaled deeply. While it was much fainter than a living person or even a corpse, a hint of that same tantalizing Smell wafted up from the meat.

Sue watched this with interest.

"This smell good," Max finally replied before realizing that didn't really answer her question. "Don't know what else to eat. Not want hurt people, but there is…Smell. Smell make us want eat."

Sue nodded along, thinking she understood.

"You're saying people smell like something you want to eat, is that right?" Sue asked delicately, trying to keep any judgement out of her voice. Max nodded miserably.

"But you say this meat smells good to you too, right? Maybe it isn't people you need, just meat," she speculated. "Or maybe…" Sue stopped mid-sentence and went over to a cupboard and pulled out a small brown jar before opening it and holding it out for Max.

He walked over and sniffed at it, and much to his surprise, a hint of The Smell came from there as well, even though whatever was in the jar certainly didn't look like meat.

"That smell okay!" Max exclaimed, the shock evident in his voice

"I think I have an idea, Max." She grinned brightly. "Lucy won't eat any meat except fish, so I've had to get creative with feeding her protein. Let's try one more."

Sue grinned at this and pulled out a small can, opened it, and held it out for Max again.

He sniffed at this too, but this time crinkled his nose slightly. Even with the diminished sense of smell he could clearly distinguish that scent. Sue laughed openly at this.

"Not many people like the smell of sardines; don't worry. Does it have that other smell, though?" Max nodded in response.

"Max, I don't think you need to eat people, or even meat. I think the smell you are talking about is somehow connected to protein."

Max stared at Sue quizzically, not quite sure he understood what she meant.

"All the things you've said have that smell have one thing in common. They are all different sources of protein. I'm no scientist of course, but maybe there is something about...*fresher* that makes it more appealing. That might explain why many of your kind that aren't so smart are so aggressive towards people. But many things have protein that aren't meat. Peanut butter, fish, beans, tofu...." Sue trailed off and laughed, clutching her stomach. Max watched her with a confused look on his face as she continued laughing, seeming to let out years worth of laughter. A moment later Chip popped his head into the room, wondering what was wrong with his mother.

"Mom, what's so funny?" Chip inquired, watching the tears of laughter that now ran down her face. He frowned a bit at this. He hadn't seen his mother laugh like this since before his dad died.

"Mom?"

Finally, Sue's laughs turned into hiccups and giggles. She wiped the tears off her face as her chuckles finally trailed off.

"Tofu zombies," she finally responded, still snorting.

Chip shook his head at his mother's oddness and went back to the den. Max just looked at her with shock, completely unsure of what had just happened. Memory recovered or not, the hilarity she had shown was an emotion Max didn't think he had felt since waking up. He then recalled dancing in the rain with Jay and smiled thinking maybe he did understand.

Sue turned to her cupboard and started looking through it as she addressed Max again. "What do you say we test this theory a bit more before we send you on your way?"

While Sue prepared the rest of the dinner, Max went to check on Jay and the children after noticing how quiet the den had gotten. On entering the empty room, he heard quiet voices coming from down the hall.

Pushing open the door, Max was greeted by a heartwarming scene.

The three were sitting on the floor in what looked like it must be Chip's room based on the spaceship models and cars littering the floor. Lucy lay on the floor, head in her hands, looking up at her brother and Jay while Chip was reading the other two a story.

Jay sat beside the Chip, watching the book in his hands intently. Jay was completely mesmerized by the boy's words. Max stood in the doorway and smiled at the domestic scene.

"And then Tommy went up, up, up to his treefort...."

A creak in the floor beneath Max caused Chip to pause and look up, grinning at him.

"I'm teaching Jay how to read!" Chip declared proudly.

"And me!" Lucy cried quickly as she turned around to see who she was informing of this important fact. "Oh, hi Max!" She jumped up and rushed over to him. "Is our dinner ready yet?"

Max looked down at the small girl and smiled fondly.

'Mom says wash hands. Go table."

Chip looked over at Jay as he stood up, offering his hand out to the less coordinated teen. Jay didn't hesitate and stood up, watching Chip intently, waiting for a clue as to what to do next.

"Come on, Jay. Mom says we gotta wash our hands. We can finish the book after dinner." Without waiting for a reaction, he pulled Jay by the hand out of the room.

Max stayed a moment longer, thinking again how sweet Jay was with all the children they had met so far. While his immediate reaction to smelling people tended to be a bit aggressive, he had maintained enough of himself to still care for the small and weak. Suddenly, Max remembered one of the conversations they had in the room before Jay had died.

Jay coughed and spat over the side of the bed away from Max before sitting back against the headboard.

"I wish I knew what happened to Dawn," Jay finally sighed, obviously lamenting more in his past, as he had been for most of the day. Max recalled the little girl he had mentioned before who lived in the house beside him.

"I told you I left after my parents died…I shoulda went to check on her too. She was such a cute kid even though she was a pain in the butt sometimes. It was kind of like having a little sister." Jay's voice cracked, both emotion and the virus running rampant in his body. "I should have saved her."

His body shook as he quietly sobbed. The guilt over leaving his parents had been on his mind often in the days after he left. The more he looked back, the more he had wondered if they were like Max, or like the ones in the hall who had bitten him. And poor little Dawn. Jay almost felt like he would be better off dying, if only to alleviate his guilt.

Max couldn't help but wonder now if this personality quirk, his love of children, was a small carryover from Jay's pre-dead life. Rousing himself from his musings, he made his way back to the others to enjoy a quiet family dinner.

CHAPTER 19

Seventeen and Three had been pleasantly surprised when Clara returned to them several hours after being led away. Since she returned though, Clara had refused to speak to either of them. Suspicion over what had occurred during her solo captivity crept into their minds.

Three wondered if she had spoken to the same woman who had tried to get him to talk, and prayed Clara hadn't given away their secrets.

Clara hardly noticed the people around her, caught up in her own thoughts after everything she had just discovered. It changed everything. Like a prayer bead, she rubbed her thumb over the picture of Max in her pocket, still feeling the thrill of remembering his name.

She thought over what Rachel had told her. She still didn't know what to make of the information.

Pregnant. The word kept running through her mind.

The word still made her feel like there were more pieces of memory fluttering on the edge of her mind, just barely out of her grasp. The emotions that came with those pieces were a mix of things Clara tried to identify.

First, joy. A strange, warm sense of happiness that started in her belly and flowed throughout her entire body.

Then, fear. A deep, dark sense of dread that renders one immobile.

Finally, sadness. Pain. Loss.

Somehow, Clara was feeling all of these at the same time, even though she didn't know why.

It was this which occupied her brain as she sat staring at the ground in front of her.

Seventeen came over and sat beside her, leaning in to look at Clara's face. Her big blue doe eyes broke Seventeen's heart, and what was initially a sense of anger and urgency quickly turned into empathy. She leaned forward and put her arms around the distraught woman.

They sat like that for a while before Seventeen realized their actions were against the norm for their kind and pulled away, not wanting to attract the attention of the guards. Putting her head down, Seventeen covered her mouth and asked the question they had been dying to know since Clara got back.

"What happened?"

Clara looked over at Seventeen before facing forward again. She considered her options for a moment.

"Nothing," Clara responded flatly. Seventeen glared at her.

"We help you. Tell us what happened."

Clara sat silently for a few more minutes before responding. "The doctor do test. Ask questions."

She did appreciate what Seventeen and Three had done for her, but also didn't know what to say or who to trust. She knew they would never believe Rachel's intentions and would think there was something more to it. Both of them hated the uninfected, and honestly, Clara didn't blame them. It was only her intuition and sense of Rachel that made her feel she could be trusted, and there was no way that the others would ever consider that enough.

Standing up, Seventeen walked back over to Three and whispered something in his ear. While he didn't react outwardly, he said something back to Seventeen that she obviously didn't like. She growled and went to sit with some of the stupids, including Nine, still glaring at her and Three.

Ignoring this display, Three just stared at Clara another moment before joining her.

"Woman doctor, right?" he asked bluntly, remembering his own experiences. Clara nodded sharply.

"Ask question, try to make talk, right?" Clara tensed but nodded again, guessing where this line of inquiry was going. "Did it work?"

Clara knew she couldn't lie her way through it anyway, but Three had read her face before she had time to respond. He inhaled sharply but didn't say anything. Clara hung her head, ashamed that she had given herself away knowing he hadn't.

She decided to try to elaborate further, explain herself.

"I pregnant. Baby inside," Clara whispered by way of explanation, putting on hand on her still flat stomach.

After several long minutes of silence, Three simply offered his hand out to her, much like she had done for him just the day before. Smiling lightly, Clara understood the peace offering for what it was and took his hand. They sat like that for the rest of the night, lost in their individual thoughts, not even caring if the soldiers saw them.

———————

Clara woke the next morning with Three still beside her. He sat alert, and she doubted he had slept. She had been noticing that he tended to take naps during the day when all their caged brethren were awake, and assumed it was so he could keep watch over them in the night.

Seventeen leaned against Nine, asleep, and Clara vowed to make things right with her today. Although they had all only known one another for a short time, a bond bred in captivity was born and further strengthened by the intelligence that separated them from their infected peers. Strife between such a minority was something Clara instinctively knew should be avoided.

A short time later, Clara heard the familiar clanging of buckets that indicated it was their feeding time. Frenzy overcame many of the caged occupants as soon as the familiar odors and clanging of the buckets hit them. They seemed to be fed every two days and while Clara was certainly hungry by this point it wasn't unbearable, just not ideal. It made her wonder of what other differences there were between before and now. The soldiers opened the gate and carelessly tossed in the buckets, which were quickly jumped on.

Clara watched as some of the soldiers started to make a game of sticking their prods through the rungs to make the captives have to jump back from the buckets each time. Laughter filled the air as the soldiers mocked the hungry infected.

Anger overwhelmed Clara at seeing them being teased and mocked in this way. When one of the soldiers actually struck someone, eliciting a loud yelp, Clara reacted without thinking.

Rushing forward she grabbed one of the prods still sticking through the grate and pulled it towards her. The unexpected action caught the soldier off guard and his face slammed into the cage as he lost his grip on the prod. He cried out as he hit the floor.

The room was stilled instantly. Clara stepped back into the center of the cage, her soiled robe flowing around her, as a low growl pick up in her throat. Her newly acquired cattle prod sat comfortably in her hand. A few drops of blood fell from the soldier's nose and the infected, excited by the momentary success and the sight of blood, started to whoop and holler around her.

The soldiers looked at one another, unsure of what to do as they watched the cage go wild, Clara's malevolent stare unnerving them further. The soldiers whispered amongst themselves and she grinned broadly at their unease.

Suddenly the door opened behind them.

A voice rang out over the commotion. "Problems, gentlemen?" The soldiers stilled and moved aside to make a path.

Captain Wolfe strode into the room and it was immediately apparent to Clara that, unlike the other soldiers, this man was a true threat. Despite her growing nervousness, she stood her ground as she watched him approach. The infected around her quieted down, oblivious to a degree, yet still aware of the change of dynamic within the room.

They could sense that their companion, the blonde with the cattle prod, was no longer the dominant force in the room.

Wolfe inspected the scene with a look of apparent disinterest and annoyance before turning back to his men. "I can't even trust you to keep watch over a bunch of stupid zombies now?" Wolfe mocked.

Private Brody, who still had blood dripping from his nose, cleared his throat. "Beg your pardon, Sir, but this one ain't so stupid." He nodded his head towards Clara, who only then realized she had just completely outed herself to the soldiers with her actions. The blood rushed from her face and her heart started pounding.

Wolfe looked her over with a smirk, "Yes, Private, I can see that." Pulling out his gun, he casually approached the cage and nodded at one of the men to open the door. He never took his eyes off Clara.

Wolfe entered the cage arrogantly, gun held casually at his side. He strutted straight up to Clara, obviously not concerned with the other occupants, who were all warily watching this exchange. A few low growls were heard, but no one moved except Wolfe.

For what seemed like forever to Clara, he stared down at her, as though trying to figure her out. His face remained impassive.

After another minute he held out his hand.

Clara froze, not sure of what to do.

She knew that, even if she shocked him, the other men would be on her in a second. Wolfe would be down for a moment, but likely wouldn't die, whereas her own chances of survival were not so good. She thought of the little one in her belly and of Max, then placed the cattle prod into his outstretched hand.

Wolfe's signature smirk reappeared as he addressed the soldiers, still looking straight at Clara. "Take control of your wards, Private. And keep a close eye on this one."

A moment later, he exited the cage and left, leaving Clara to wonder what the ramifications would be of what she'd just done.

She felt a hand grab her own and felt a reassuring squeeze from Seventeen. She squeezed back gratefully. Whatever would happen, they were in this together.

CHAPTER 20

Dinner had gone better than Max expected. While he and Jay both certainly left a bit to be desired in the realm of table manners, Max was delighted to see Jay heartily eat his steaks. He was equally pleased with having a full belly himself and enjoyed the meal despite it not being fresh. There was a peaceful sense of normality that came with dinner at a table, and he glowed with warmth and content.

Chip and Lucy were obviously thrilled to have new faces around their dinner table, and Sue seemed to be lighter overall watching her children's happiness.

After they had all finished, Chip and Lucy pulled out one of their board games and were attempting to teach Jay how to play. It was some strange children's game involving trapping little balls in colorful animals' mouths. Jay didn't seem to grasp that the point of the game wasn't to just press the button to make its mouth open again and again, despite the children's best efforts to teach him. Nevertheless, he was delighted by it, and his odd version of giggles made everyone laugh. Soon the children gave up trying to play the game and Lucy directed a small story created on the spot, prompting her brother and Jay to move their mouths along with the story.

Max watched this all with a tinge of sadness. Seeing how well Jay got along here, he knew it wasn't going to be easy to leave. He couldn't help but wonder if he should leave him here and continue to find Clara on his own. *Would he be better off with them?*

Sue came up behind him and leaned over to ask him if he could watch them while she checked their food stores in the crawlspace. Before he had even registered she was approaching, *The Smell* hit Max's senses. While it was a controllable craving, it was also against his instincts that he didn't act.

Max then realized that, even with a full belly, his kind would always be a danger to the uninfected. With Jay having even less mental capacity, there would never be a guarantee he wouldn't be a threat to Sue and her children.

Max murmured his assent to Sue who didn't seem to notice the sudden melancholy that had overcome him. She wandered to the back of the house, completely trusting of the two zombies watching her children.

Max looked at Chip and Lucy, thought about Sue and her kindness, and knew he could never risk leaving Jay here. While he truly didn't think that Jay would ever hurt them, he could never be sure, and wouldn't be able to live with himself if he thought the kind family might be in danger.

With resolve, he stood up to go find Sue and ask her again if she had thought of a faster way to get him across the country to Clara.

"He actually taught you how to read the sun before he died?" Sue exclaimed, impressed at Jay's idea. Max nodded, also proud of Jay's foresight. He wouldn't have gotten this far if not for him, and he would forever be in Jay's debt. Not only for helping him escape the room and learn to speak, but also for the brilliant ideas the boy had shown in planning their journey across the country.

"Well, since we live in Canada, rain is obviously going to happen, and with it, clouds. It's early enough in the fall that we may still have nice weather ahead, but we can't guarantee it, and going across the prairies will certainly be a gamble." Sue rambled on.

She had pulled out a map of Canada, a lucky remnant of one of Chip's school projects, and was thinking of ways her new friends would possibly be able to make it across. Max stared at the map with interest but tried not to interrupt Sue's train of thought.

Suddenly, she straightened up and walked towards the front door. Max followed, curious of the sudden call to action.

Pressing her ear against the door, Sue listened for a moment before entering the store. She quickly moved to the front and pulled a road map off a rack and rushed back into the apartment, closing the door behind her.

Grinning, she looked at Max. "I have an idea!"

———

Two days later, Sue's plan was ready to go. With Jay distracting the children, she had taught Max the basics of reading a map and using a compass. He would no longer need to rely on the sun to find out where they were going. While he hadn't yet figured out reading, she also showed him how to match letters to compare words.

Sue's best idea, however, had come when they had been reviewing the route that seemed best for directness without as much human, or even other infected, interference. It was then they found the train. It was a route that went almost straight across the country,

Unsure if it would still be making its cross-country route, Sue also took the time to teach Max the basics of how to operate a car using one of Chips toys. The basics of key, pedal, and wheel, anyway. If it was in more open areas, he should be able to figure out a vehicle well enough. The train would be the best scenario, but Sue and Max agreed it would be best to avoid people going forward; not everyone would be as accepting as their family had been.

There was no way to determine if or how they would get on the train, whether it would stop somewhere they could get on it, and all the other factors. If nothing else, they found that if Max and Jay followed the tracks it was a relatively direct and hopefully easy way to guide them across the country. Max was incredibly grateful for everything Sue had done and came up with a plan to help the family that had been so helpful.

"Out of the question, Max! It is way too dangerous out there, and we have enough food to last a few weeks, at least!" Sue argued. She and Max had been fighting the entire evening before.

Max, however, was not to be dissuaded.

He knew Sue wouldn't risk leaving the kids alone to find supplies. The least he could do for them after Jay and his abrupt entrance into their lives was ensure they had food. Then a better barrier at the front of the store.

Once Sue gave up arguing about him leaving, she tried to convince him to take her bat to protect himself, the one real weapon they had. Once again, Max refused.

Had Clara been there, she would have told Sue that Max was stubborn, and once he set his mind to something, it was almost impossible to talk him out of it.

Leaving Jay with the children was also a request he made, not wanting to worry about him while he looked for supplies. Max was hoping for quickness and stealth, neither being very realistic with a shambling teen following him. Despite Sue's misgivings about Max being in the outside world on his own, she understood it would be safer to leave Jay and quickly agreed to let him stay with her and the children.

The next morning, Max set off on his own back onto the gloomy streets of Toronto.

CHAPTER 21

The compound was quiet, sedated by the lateness of the hour. Downstairs, the infected slept, and only a few soldiers remained awake to keep watch over their sleeping comrades.

Rachel left her room and shut the door quietly behind her before moving down the hall. Guards and soldiers still patrolled, and while she had a pretty good idea of where what she needed would be located, she knew timing this perfectly was key. Curiosity and a desire to help drove her forward, despite the very real knowledge that if she followed through with her plans it would be considered treason.

Creeping down the halls feeling very much like a criminal, she made her way towards Wolfe's office.

Rachel heard about the earlier display of aggression in the holding area, and by the description she had been given—"Blonde smarter one with the fuzzy robe"—she knew that it was Clara. While Rachel didn't have access to the security footage, she imagined the woman must have been provoked in some way to have reacted in that manner. She hadn't been aggressive at all with Rachel, other than the one moment she felt threatened.

After dodging a few of the guards, including a less than elegant scurry into a janitor's closet, Rachel finally arrived in front of Wolfe's office.

Luckily for her, the narcissistic asshole didn't think anyone would truly go into his office and, as such, the door was unlocked. Careful to keep the door from slamming shut, Rachel crept into the room, keeping the lights off in case anyone wandered by at this late hour. Sweat ran down her neck. She had never really been one for breaking the rules and she could feel her heart pounding in her throat.

Making her way over to the desk, she prayed it would be unlocked like the door had been and was quickly rewarded for her prayers.

He really doesn't think anyone would come in here, does he? she mused as she pulled out the records she was looking for.

Since the beginning, the soldiers had been instructed to make a note of where every infected they picked up had come from. This had been on another researcher's suggestion, figuring that they may eventually be able to use the data to differentiate aspects of the virus based on location and other factors. Rachel hoped that the ones who had picked up Clara had filled out their paperwork.

Flipping through, she finally found the reports from the few that had been picked up in Vancouver. Obviously, there weren't names, but luckily for her, only three female zombies had been in the van with Clara, and one of them was listed as being black prior to infection, leaving only two addresses.

Excitement shot through Rachel as she rushed to write down the information and put the reports back in the door. Distracted, she left the reports she had copied on the top of the pile and shoved them back in the drawer. While she didn't yet know what she was going to do with this information, she had a vague idea and knew that now was her opportunity. Making her sneaky exit, she went back to her room to silently celebrate her success.

Captain Jeffrey Wolfe sat in his private quarters with a small screen in his lap, watching the cage with interest. Luckily for Rachel, he hadn't switched views in a while, intent on watching the zombies. In particular after the day's events.

Despite what he had told the doctor, he absolutely had special interest in the smart zombies he knew she was studying. Not only did they not feel pain, but they also seemed to be stronger, impervious to cold and, hopefully, malleable enough to be the perfect soldier.

Wolfe stared at the screen, watching the blonde zombie who was sitting between the old man and the black zombie, all holding hands like some little nursery. That made him chuckle.

In a few days' time, his current round of private 'experiments' would be complete, and he would be ready for a new specimen. This time, he wanted to see the true capability of the smarter ones, and Wolfe knew he could be much more persuasive than the doctor.

CHAPTER 22

Max made his way down the lifeless streets, keeping in mind shops and landmarks as he passed so he could find his way back. Most of the shops seemed to have broken windows and the post-virus wreckage was evident everywhere he went. The rain had washed away most of the blood, leaving only wet debris and corpses behind. The smell of rot was now mingling with something akin to the scent of a wet dog.

While making his plan to leave, he and Sue had decided that Max would attract less attention on foot and was more likely to find somewhere promising nearby. While keeping a slow, watchful pace, he looked for places that appeared like they would contain a decent amount of food for Sue and the children.

After a while, he began to feel like he was being watched and stopped to look around. Noticing a slight movement from his right, he slowly approached the alley to investigate. When he was only ten or so feet away, a filthy brown dog jumped out from behind a garbage can and growled at Max. Unsure of what to do, Max stood still, and a moment later the animal barked loudly at him before running off. Not wanting to waste time in pursuing it, Max continued on.

He came across a grocery store about ten minutes later, and while the door was broken, it looked like there was still a lot left. Max thought he heard something behind him, but scanning the parking lot he saw nothing.

Deciding he didn't want to be surprised by anything, he poked his head inside the door and looked around. Seeing nothing in the dimly lit shop, he shouted, "Ahhhhhhh!!!!" He kept his ears open for any sound of movement and one foot out the door in case he needed to bolt. Nothing. He tried once more.

"Hellloooo?"

Again, silence greeted him.

Staying at the front of the store, he walked along the aisles, peering down each of them. Many of the shelves and racks had been tossed around, but Max couldn't yet see any signs of blood or anything more than the typical whiffs he got outdoors of the uninfected. Satisfied there was no immediate threat, he started down the first aisle, pleased to see he was correct; a lot of food remained on the shelves. It seemed that a benefit of the fast-moving virus, at least for the survivors, was the lack of time people had to loot.

Since his reading ability hadn't returned, Sue had shown him some of the non-perishable food she had in the house so he would know what to look for. With that in mind, he pulled out one of the backpacks he brought and started loading it with cans. Quickly noticing the backpack was getting heavy, he moved down the aisle to other dry foods, like noodles and rice, which Sue had also shown him. He quickly finished filling one backpack and went and placed it by the front door before grabbing the second and returning to the aisles to fill it.

As he wandered down another aisle to see what else was left, he heard a noise coming from the back of the store. He warily placed the backpack down on the floor and stayed completely still, listening to see if the noise would repeat itself. After a moment, it happened again, and seemed to be coming from behind some doors off to his right.

Max looked around for a weapon, but only found a broom. Picking it up, he approached the doors while holding the broom out of in front of him. Using the long handle, he slowly pushed the doors open and waited.

Silence.

Taking a deep breath, he stepped into the back room, waiting a moment for his eyes to adjust to the even dimmer lighting. He quickly found the source of the sound. In front of him, an infected man sat staring blankly at the floor while scratching absently at the ground beside him. The man didn't seem to be injured but was so insentient he barely seemed alive.

Scratch – scratch – scratch.

"Hello?" Max inquired, slowly approaching. The man gave no reaction to Max's voice.

When he was a few feet away, Max stopped and knelt, looking the man over.

Based on the pale skin and dirty appearance, Max knew the man was like him; however, the blank look on his face rivaled even Jay. The man didn't seem to be aware of anything around him. Suddenly, a slight grumble came from the man and Max quickly moved back before realizing it was coming from his stomach. He chuckled to himself.

"Hungry, friend?" Max inquired rhetorically. "I be back." He stood up and walked back through the heavy swinging doors in search of something to eat.

Based on Sue's revelation about protein, he decided to look for cans he could open easily that had some kind of animal on them. He figured that would be the best way to determine what would be good without being able to read the labels or having to smell them.

Wandering through the aisles, he finally found some small cans with tabs on the top and small felines on the label. Testing them, he opened one, pleased it was easy to open and that it had the smell he now associated with protein. *Perfect*, he thought to himself.

He made his way back to his new acquaintance bearing gifts of cat food.

In the back room of the wrecked grocery store, Max opened half a dozen cans of cat food and sat down beside the infected man, who immediately accepted his offering. Other than the slurping sounds the man made, they enjoyed their meal in shared silence.

As Max ate, he considered the man at his side, who seemed to be capable of feeding himself when food was presented, but otherwise remained unchanged.

Even at the beginning, Jay had more sense of humanity than this, Max thought. He thought about the different infected he had met so far and the varying degrees of intelligence and memory they had shown. While he was the only one he knew of who could really speak, it seemed there was more variation than he first anticipated. As he watched the man finish off his third can of cat food, he wondered what Clara would be like when he got back to her.

Would she still be healthy, hiding in their home like Sue? Or did the virus infect her too? If it did, would she be hungry and angry? Slow and stupid? Or maybe, just maybe, would she be like Max? Considering the number of people he had met so far and knowing none were quite like him, he felt as though the odds were against him. Sighing, he handed the rest of his cans over to the other man, who quickly devoured them with every evidence of enjoyment.

"I go back, need get more food for others. I come back to you," Max told the other man, who didn't even look up much less acknowledge his statement as he licked the bottoms of the cans to get every remnant of food out.

Max wandered back into the shop and went back to filling the second backpack, making a point to fill a third extra one with the cans they had just eaten for Jay and himself to take on their upcoming journey. Knowing they contained some kind of cat protein and that they were easy to open made them an ideal food for infected-on-the-go. He was so engrossed in his task he almost didn't notice the back room doors swing inwards towards the back. Seeing this, he wondered if his new acquaintance had just joined him, but couldn't see his head over the aisles.

Curious, he put the bags down and walked to the back, only to find the man still sitting exactly where he left him.

Frowning, Max looked around.

"You move, friend…?" He began to ask when a large furry body slammed into his, crashing him into the ground. Max's instincts kicked in and he quickly brought his arms up to his face as he wrestled with the heaving, snarling body of the dog that had been following him. Keeping his forearm over the dog's throat, he strained to keep the sharp teeth from his face but was quickly losing his strength.

Suddenly he felt the weight of the dog lift off him and looked up to see his acquaintance hurl the rabid dog across the room. The man growled at the dog, who got up shaking his head. The dog snarled back completely unphased, furious at the intruder who had interrupted his hunt.

Max watched paralyzed by fear and surprise, as the two adversaries stared at one another, readying themselves for the attack. Even though he was watching closely, the moment they both sprang at one another happened so suddenly that Max felt as though he didn't even see them start to move.

As he watched the once-stationary infected man, he was amazed at the speed with which he attacked the animal. The two rolled and struggled, growling at one another until finally the man got a grip on the animal's head and stunned it by slamming its head against the concrete flooring. One more solid hit and the animal was done, its bowels emptying onto the floor.

In an instant, the infected man's demeanor changed again. A small whine in his throat could be heard as he shuffled over to Max and went down on his knees, his head hung low to his chest. For a moment Max couldn't move, still stunned by what had just happened.

"You save me," Max finally croaked. The infected man whined again before Max realized he was looking for…acceptance? Approval? He wasn't sure, but the posture reminded him of when Jay had done things he knew Max didn't like.

"It okay," Max coaxed as he stood up and wiped away the dog drool that still covered his face. Helping his infected savior up, he led him back over to the pallets where they had been sitting previously. Still the man refused to lift his head and look at Max.

Unsure of what else to do, Max opened another can of cat food and handed it to him. The man took it slowly and mindlessly put the food into his mouth. Max watched this with interest before carefully grabbing the man's chin and lifting his head until his eyes to meet his own.

A bit of sadness lay behind those blue cloudy eyes, but mostly just a glazed, far off look. Dropping his chin, Max let the man finish his meal as he sat down beside him.

"Thank you," Max finally whispered, not actually expecting a response. Still not reacting, the man finished his cat food and curled up on the ground beside Max and closed his eyes. Unsure of what else to do, Max joined him.

Max opened his eyes an indeterminate amount of time later to find that the other man was no longer beside him. Sitting up, he looked around and noticed the dog was also missing. With concern, he stood to get a better look before hearing some faint rustling noises from further down the large store room.

Max moved cautiously towards the noises. After a moment, he looked behind one of the stacks of pallets and found what looked like a large nest in a concealed corner of the room. The infected man had clearly been sleeping here for a while, which was evident by the scraps of food and clothing that littered the floor.

The man himself was occupied, covering up the corpse of the dog. Whether for burial or a later snack Max couldn't tell, but noticing the blood on the man's chin that hadn't been there before, he could take a guess. Not being one to judge, Max left the man to his business and went back into the store, determined to finally complete his mission.

A short time later, he had the last backpack filled with dried and canned food, which he put by the front of the store with the rest. Finished with what he had set out to do, Max debated what to do with his infected rescuer. While the man seemed timid, it certainly hadn't taken him long to jump into action either. He also didn't seem to respond to any basic instruction and Max assumed the protection was his rudimentary method of thanks for the food. Or perhaps it was just a rudimentary survival instinct. Max would never know for sure.

Max went back to the nest, unsure of what he planned to do. Hunching down beside him, Max stared at the man, who still sat almost completely motionless except for the mindless scratching on the ground, which he seemed to favor. Sighing, Max looked at the pathetic soul and knew he couldn't just leave him.

Max pulled the man to his feet, getting no resistance as he led him towards the front of the store. First putting two backpacks on himself, he carefully loaded the third onto the infected man's back as he just stood there. Max started to step out the door, his arm holding onto the infected arm, ready to get them back to Sue's. He figured he would leave him at the front of Sue's shop while dropping off the loot and grabbing Jay, thus not exposing Sue and the children to the unpredictable man.

Before he could get more than a foot out the door, the man ripped his arm from Max's grasp and practically leapt back into the store.

Max stared back at him in shock, once again amazed at the speed with which this man moved despite his outwardly zombie-like appearance. He walked back in beside the man, who stood just inside the door.

"You come with Max. Keep safe. Bring to friends," Max tried to explain, but the man gave no indication he understood. Deciding to try once more, he gently grabbed the man's arm, only to have the man pull it from Max's grasp immediately, this time letting out a small whine.

Not willing to force the man, Max removed the backpack and watched as he immediately turned towards the back of the store. Max watched his slow progression through the aisles until he went through the swinging doors and into the back room. Not wasting another moment, Max took the third backpack in his hands and walked back out down the road, leaving the infected man to his store and solitude.

CHAPTER 23

The next morning, Rachel had done her best to act like everything was normal. She pored over the information in Clara's file, which wasn't much, and memorized the address where the woman had been taken. She realized that it was over an hour's drive from the base, closer to the city, and Rachel wondered what the soldiers had been doing so far off course.

The longer Rachel stayed at the compound and the more she learned, she felt as though there was something else going on. Many things weren't adding up, and it was making her uneasy to not know all the parts currently at play here. As a scientist, she put a lot of weight into the facts of any matter. Not having so much of the information available didn't sit right with her.

There was Wolfe's strange reactions towards her experiments, and the hidden knowledge of them having already discovered the smarter version of zombie, plus the strange route Rachel noticed they had captured Clara on, and so many other things. Rachel was getting suspicious, but of what, she didn't quite know yet.

"You seem a bit distracted today," Shannon, one of Rachel's colleagues, commented. Rachel looked down and realized she had been stirring the same cup of instant coffee for several minutes. Her face reddened.

"Yeah, I guess I'm just not feeling great today." At her words, Shannon immediately walked over and put her hand to Rachel's forehead.

"No fever. You followed protocol for the exams, right? I know we think we're immune, but you need to be careful. Not enough of us virologists left that we can afford you to be getting sick," Shannon chastised. Rachel smiled at her friend's concern.

"Don't worry, I've been careful. Just didn't get much sleep last night."

"Okay, if you're sure."

"Actually, do you mind keeping an eye on things here? I think an afternoon off wouldn't go amiss."

Shannon quickly agreed and shooed Rachel from their lab. Free for the remainder of the day, she wandered the facility, something she previously had no reason to do.

In most areas, there was a guard or two kicking around, with anywhere from two to six in the cage room at any given time. It wasn't until she went to the east wing that she had any troubles.

Three very alert guards stood outside a set of heavy steel doors similar to those of her lab. Curious, she approached them, assuming a nonchalant attitude.

Without hesitation, she walked by them as if to enter the doors, and immediately two of the men raised their guns, with the third placing himself directly in front of her, frowning.

"No civilian access, Miss," the one in front of her stated.

Batting her eyes, Rachel held up her badge indicating she was a head researcher.

"Oh, I understand, but I'm not a civilian. I'm Captain Wolfe's top researcher." She followed this with a brilliant toothy smile. Seeing this have no effect, she took a gamble. "The Captain asked me to check in on…the other samples. He said they were here and to get you fine gentlemen to let me in since he doesn't have time to come down himself."

Still frowning, the three men looked at one another for a moment before one of them spoke up. "There's no way she could know what we have in there unless he told her," idiot guard number three conceded as he stepped aside. The others grumbled their consent, much to Rachel's astonishment. Trying not to let her surprise show, she thanked them and quickly went through the door before they realized their mistake.

As soon as she went through, Rachel realized she had entered into a connecting room, sealing off what looked like a laboratory by sheets of plastic and another set of doors. As she stepped forward, several smells assaulted her senses.

Bleach.

Disinfectant.

Blood.

Decay.

Taking a breath through her mouth, she pushed through the plastic and the doors and gasped at the sight in front of her.

Rows of gurneys lined an entire wall, a zombie tied down to each in varying states of decay. Rather than the usual equipment that would adorn the room, such as medical or research tools, she saw what looked more like torture devices.

Knives, scalpels, and bone saws were things she would expect to see in a room like this. The blowtorch, nails, drill, and other nasty objects strewn around, not so much.

She slowly made her way down the room, looking over the bodies left to rot. Each one was truly dead, thankfully. Based on the amount of blood that covered the room, she assumed they had been alive before the damage had been done. She shuddered and moved forward.

A thousand thoughts flew through Rachel's head as she stood there looking at the utter destruction with horror. *They were living people*, she thought. *Infected, stupid, dangerous…yes. But still human.*

Rachel thought back to her earlier findings and remembered having told Wolfe about how the virus manipulated and dulled pain receptors. It seemed the captain might be testing that theory. She prayed for the sake of those lying dead before her that she had been correct.

Then she thought of the blonde woman and the baby growing inside her against all odds. What would Wolfe and his men do to them if they found out they had a captive pregnant zombie?

From another room at the end of the row she heard a loud growl and a banging noise, breaking her from her reverie.

Rachel quickly turned to leave rather than looking to see what was making the noise. Anything in this area was obviously not something she wanted to see. She rushed past the soldiers on her way out, not even giving them a backwards glance.

She couldn't let this happen to the rest of them, especially the woman she had grown an unlikely bond with. One way or another, she would get them out.

The next morning, Rachel did her best to continue her act of normality. After breakfast—lukewarm oatmeal and a vitamin pill—she made her way back downstairs to the cage.

"I need to see blonde woman again," Rachel declared without preamble. "We need to run some more tests."

Private Brody, who now wore a bandage over his busted nose, looked Rachel up and down slowly, causing her to blush and the men around him to chuckle. "I don't know, sweet doctor," He began patronizingly. "We were told to keep an extra special watch on that one. Maybe you need some, uhh, company." Open laughter around her as he leaned in, crowding her space.

Rachel, albeit beet red, stood her ground to the condescending soldier. "I think I'll be fine, thanks." She moved forward out of his reach and stood beside the cage door, arms crossed over her chest. Smirking, he complied, and fifteen minutes later Rachel and Clara were back in her private lab.

Clara looked around the room, less fearful and more curious this time. She still couldn't explain why she trusted the doctor, but she did. After a moment, she looked over at Rachel, who was fiddling with her lab coat and seemed to be distracted, staring at a spot on the papers in front of her.

Clara gently put her hand onto the Rachel's, causing her to look up into her infected blue eyes.

"Baby?" Clara inquired first, wondering if it was okay or if the tests had revealed anything. Much to her relief, Rachel instantly shook her head. "No," she began, "the baby seems to be fine. There isn't any way to know if it will have the virus, but it shows no signs of distress. I erased all the records of the tests we did, switched them for others so no one would find out." Rachel stopped, hesitating on her next words.

Clara waited patiently for the doctor to finish.

"You are fine now," Rachel continued, "but I don't think you will be for long. Whatever you did in front of Wolfe obviously got you noticed. I am sure you can appreciate why that isn't a good thing."

At this, Clara nodded. She expected as much after it happened but didn't understand why the doctor cared or why she was telling her. She wasn't going to turn away the help, in any case.

"What do?" Clara asked simply. Sighing deeply, Rachel looked her in the eye and told her. "I am going to get you out of here and back to Max."

CHAPTER 24

Max spent the next few hours carefully and quietly making his way back to Sue's. Luckily his return journey was mostly uneventful, though he saw a stray dog down one alley and quickly moved on, intent on avoiding further animal altercations.

Staying at a slower pace, he continued thinking about everything that had happened since leaving the hotel room. So far, other than Sue and the kids, every encounter he had with anyone, or anything, had ended in death. The bloodshed was wearing him down and he desperately hoped they could make it back to Clara without further incidents.

Before he knew it, Max was back at the store knocking on Sue's door as they had discussed. Max had insisted that they barricade the door from the inside after he left. The family had been lucky once, but Max knew that the next infected to cross their paths likely wouldn't be like him.

Knock. Knock-knock. Knock.

A moment later, her heard a small voice call out. "Max, is that you!?" Max smiled at hearing Lucy's sweet voice.

"Yes, Lucy. Get Sue open door for me?" He heard the quick patter of tiny feet and a few moments later he was back in the familiar apartment.

As soon as he was in though, Max got to receive his first dose of feminine wrath since his awakening. "What the hell were you thinking staying out all night and making us worry? I was worried sick! You can't do that to people, Max. We had no clue where you.." Sue trailed off as she noticed the growing smile on Max's face.

"And what the hell are you smiling about? I was beside myself, thinking the worst, and so were the kids and Jay!"

Max just continued smiling for a moment. Finally, he responded simply: "Sue care about Max." At this, Sue stopped her rant and smirked at him.

"Yeah, I care, you big dummy. Now get in here and tell me what happened."

Awhile later Max had recounted his story, helped Sue pack away the food, and was now sitting listening to Chip read to Jay and Lucy again. They had all been interested, but not overly surprised regarding his revelations about the varying degrees of humanity in the infected. Jay and Max were already examples of the variety of the infected, and the fact that there were more variations wasn't shocking. Sue had cackled at the cat food included in the bags, but in hearing Max's explanation of why he picked it agreed it had made sense. She decided not to tell him that cans with cats on them contained food *for* cats and was not made *of* cats, like he assumed.

Lying back in his chair, Max closed his eyes and listened to the small boy's voice, letting it wash over him. Chip was now recounting how, while Max was gone, he had tried to teach Jay to ride his bike, wanting to help them in their journey after hearing his mother and Max talking about it.

"It was *SO* funny, Max! He would just sit there and put his feet on the pedals and just fall to the side. He just wouldn't pedal at all and just kept falling! And that's why he has scrapes all over his face." Chip finished on a laugh. Jay sat beside the boy with a smile on his face and, despite the numerous cuts covering his cheeks, he seemed pleased with himself. Max chuckled at the image of how it had happened and thanked Chip for his efforts.

Part of him wanted to stay. Sue and the kids really had been like a little family to them. They had taken in two zombies not knowing what would happen, and the care and kindness they had shown gave Max hope for the future and for people like him. He hated that people saw him as a monster, a zombie.

Nevertheless, he knew that at some point he had promised Clara he would come home to her. While he couldn't remember why or when, he knew that it was a promise he would never break. As much as he adored Sue, Chip, and Lucy, it was time for him and Jay to go.

The next day, Sue approached Max first thing in the morning and handed him two bags. Without needing to be told, she knew. As much as she hated to see them go, she knew the smiles and light they brought to her and her children would stay with them. They had brought hope and friendship, and Sue would cherish that. She also understood what was driving Max. Hearing his story and the passion with which he spoke about Clara, it made her heart ache for her late husband and she understood that same love drove Max. Until he found Clara, or found out what happened to her, he would never be at peace.

Both Lucy and Chip cried when they saw Max preparing them to go. Sue hugged them both and thanked them for everything. He could have sworn he saw a tear in Jay's eyes; however, his friend didn't hesitate to follow Max when the time came. As quick as that, they were on their way again, back outside and ready to head towards the train station.

In their planning, Sue had determined it would take a couple of days walking to get to the train station, where they hoped to catch a ride. Arming Max with a map and compass was the best thing she could have done for them, and he left that morning feeling ready for anything.

Max hadn't wanted to take any potential weapons from the family, but now that he realized even animals could pose a threat, he decided that would be their first stop. Luckily, the post-viral chaos left a number of readily available options strewn about the streets. In Canada, there were far fewer guns than may have been available had they been a bit further south; however, Max was perfectly happy with the tire iron he found just outside the shop. Its sturdy form yet light weight appealed to him. Besides, he had no idea how to work any kind of firearm and didn't think now was the time to learn.

For the first few hours, Jay seemed particularly sullen. Although he hadn't really spoken since he turned, his body language and face seemed to be more expressive almost daily since his awakening and Max had a pretty good idea of what was bothering him.

"Jay-man?" Jay turned to Max at hearing his name, but didn't try to say anything, just stared at his mentor. A twang of guilt struck Max.

"Thank you," Max continued, "for coming with me." Even if the teen didn't completely understand, Max truly hoped he knew how grateful he was. Being in the hotel room had taught Max loneliness, and it wasn't a feeling that he wanted to repeat.

Jay stopped his depressed shamble and looked up at Max, staring right into his eyes.

"Clara," he said, before continuing down the road.

Max stood there stunned for a moment before following after his friend. His shoulders felt lighter knowing that Jay understood and was with him as they continued down the abandoned streets of the city.

Another few hours passed before Max decided that, between their grumbling bellies and the waning light of day, they should find a place to stop soon. They had made good progress, but still had a good two days ahead of them before he expected to see the train.

Realizing by now that outward appearances meant little when identifying an uninhabited place, Max decided to try a new tactic. He would look for somewhere that wouldn't have been a popular looting spot. He reasoned that food or supplies meant people, and Max still intended to avoid people. Jay gave no further insight after his singular word earlier and plodded along behind Max.

Finally settling on what used to be a print and copy store that was left unlocked and unlooted, the two made their way to the back room and shared a dinner of cat food before curling up to sleep.

Max woke with a start and immediately looked beside him to see Jay was not there. Frantically, he searched the store, but couldn't find the teen anywhere; however, his backpack was still there. Assuming he couldn't have gone far, Max left their things and rushed outside. He immediately saw Jay standing a few shops down, staring at a bike that was leaning against a post, apparently forgotten in someone's haste.

Relieved his friend was okay, Max approached Jay, who still stared at his find.

"Jay like bike?" Max inquired, smiling a bit. At this Jay turned to Max as though finally realizing he was standing there and pointed at the bicycle with a small inquiring moan. Max considered the distance they still had to go to get to the train and wondered if there might be something to this bike thing. A vague memory of a saying floated through his head about not forgetting how to ride a bike. If they could find one more bike, which shouldn't be hard, then they could maybe even get to the train station later today. If they could learn how to ride, that is.

"We can try," Max finally acquiesced, earning him a smile from Jay. "But Chip told me about last time. You wear this." Max handed him the helmet that was attached to the bars.

"Let's see what we can do."

A few hours later, Max understood the dilemma that Chip had gone through, as well as the hilarity. While Jay certainly had the drive to learn how, the overall mechanics of the bike seemed too great for his simple mind.

Max clutched his belly and laughed as Jay fell off once again, grateful for his foresight in the helmet. Each time he fell, Jay didn't seem to mind, though. Max had already guessed that pain processing had somehow changed for their kind. However, he also understood that in itself could be dangerous as well. Max had tried to ride it and, while he was able to do it to a rudimentary degree, his reaction time wasn't great and he didn't have much confidence in how much faster it would really be.

After trying to help Jay get on and pedal for the dozenth time, he finally accepted that less capable infected like Jay could not ride bikes.

While it had been a failure, it had been fun for both of them. Max grabbed their bags and opened a few cans of cat food, which they both ate with gusto before preparing themselves to move onwards.

Max pulled out the map to check where they were, before confirming their route for the day. Luckily for them, Sue's house was located in almost a straight line to where they were going, so as long as Max kept an eye on the streets (he still couldn't read the signs but could match the letters well enough) and watched the sun, he had confidence they wouldn't get lost. Based on what Sue had calculated, they should reach the trains by the next day.

CHAPTER 25

"Out?!" Seventeen whispered loudly, immediately being shushed by Three. Clara nodded.

After Rachel had informed Clara of her intention, she immediately asked that the rest of her caged counterparts be freed and that Three and Seventeen be allowed to come wherever Clara went. She knew this was the least she could do for the two of them to thank them for their support since being captured. If Nine or any of the other semi-smarts were able to, they could follow. Rachel had reluctantly agreed to release everyone but couldn't guarantee how many she could get out of the compound safely. Clara understood this was a risk for all involved; however, so was staying and doing nothing. Once again, her hand moved to her belly.

Clara looked at Three to see what his response would be, knowing that Seventeen would go along with whatever he decided. No emotion or decision showed on his face, and Clara wondered what the man was thinking.

"Very dangerous," he finally said. Clara nodded again. That much was obvious. Seventeen, unable to sit still anymore waiting for his decision, got up and paced the cage, ignoring the constant frenzy around them. After a few moments, Clara was beginning to get antsy as well, before Three opened his mouth again to ask one question: "How?"

"How?" Clara asked, looking to Rachel for answers.

"I am not completely sure yet," Rachel responded honestly. "But you all need to be ready at a moment's notice. I will need some kind of distraction to get the guards away from the cage, but I don't know what yet. Releasing the rest should give us the time we need to get out."

"And friends?"

Rachel smiled at the dedication of the woman in front of her. Nodding, she replied, "just make sure they are ready to go. We can't wait for anyone, so if someone falls behind, we have to keep moving. Do you understand?"

Swallowing lightly, Clara nodded once more and put a protective arm over her belly. Yes, Clara understood. And as much as she wanted to save Three and Seventeen, her priority was right here.

Three spent the rest of the day in contemplative silence. Despite his refusal to speak to the doctor, he had gotten the sense that she wasn't the same as the other humans that were keeping them captive. Regardless, his experiences with humans so far left a lot to be desired. As much as he wanted to believe the doctor, he still felt hesitant.

Three's memories of before his awakening were limited, but he did get a sense that he was often alone even before. His sense of protection for the two women seemed familiar as well, but he held almost no memories of before he died. Sighing, he watched Seventeen comfort the pregnant woman and behind them, one of the soldiers looked their way, whispering about the interactions they were witnessing. Despite his misgivings, he decided it would be far more dangerous to stay.

While downstairs they were debating the wisdom of trusting Rachel, she was busy working on a plan to get them out. Luckily, the compound was not as well run as the previous one in Seattle, both due to lack of personnel as well as the overall layout. Trying to focus on planning, however, was proving difficult for Rachel right now. She was a scientist though, and was used to problem solving and thinking with logic. She just needed to apply the same principals to this problem.

At first, she had thought about a fire or even fire alarm, but she also worried that those inside wouldn't take it seriously. After a zombie apocalypse, it was hard to be as affected by a mere fire alarm. She thought about using a more forceful method—grabbing a few guns and seeing how far that got her. Again, the problem was that the soldiers were not very frightened of guns and were much faster and more familiar with them than she was. Could she hope to overpower them all on her own? She tried to focus on her own strengths instead. What did she have that the others didn't? What could she use to her advantage?

A few hours later, Rachel had the seed of a plan. It wasn't overly elaborate or pretty, but she prayed it would work. She began to set it to action, trying to ignore the fact that she was about to unleash a lot of infected people.

CHAPTER 26

The rest of the day they made decent progress. It was unseasonably warm for September and Max's spirits were bright despite the desolate state of the streets of Toronto. They had seen a few other small groups of infected, but none bothered them in the slightest. They did see one woman who was sitting in the middle of the street; however, she seemed to be like the man Max had met in the store. Max approached her and tried a greeting, but after a few minutes of complete unresponsiveness he gave up and continued onwards. Max noted how few people they had seen and wondered about it. Jay had told him Toronto was a large city, and while the scale of it seemed that way, the number of people they had seen didn't give that impression. There was no way of knowing the level of devastation the FIRE virus had caused around the world.

It was only a few weeks since the first signs of the virus were spotted, and in that time, it had covered the globe. FIRE was fast, deadly, and contagious, and had left no stone unturned. Of the millions of people worldwide that hadn't died from the virus, many had since died from direct infection caused by bites and the inevitable human element that came along with such massive amounts of death and destruction. The remaining population was spread out and hiding.

The effect of all of this was severalfold for Max.

First, it meant that the city was relatively quiet. While it wasn't uncommon for a few bodies to litter the streets, they hadn't seen a live person, infected or not, in hours. Second, the few people who did happen to see Max and Jay quickly hid to avoid them. The infected were widely considered savage zombies and either avoided or killed quickly and quietly. They had been lucky to meet Sue, who had given them a chance few others would have. While all did seem quiet, Max didn't notice the eyes watching them through the blinds of some of houses as they walked by.

Happy with the progress they had made, Max began to look for a place to hunker down for the night. He wasn't in much of a hurry but was keeping his eyes out for suitable places. As Max was scanning the buildings around him, a low rumble came from the ground, causing Jay to immediately start growling. Understanding that a potential threat was approaching, Max quickly pulled Jay off the street and into a nearby alley. They hid behind a dumpster but peered out from the edges, curious to see what this new thing was.

A moment later, several large trucks came into view, stopping a few yards in front of the alley. Max held Jay back, sure that whoever would come out of the vehicles wouldn't be friendly. The trucks were just out of view, but Max could hear doors slam shut and male voices float towards them. "That was fucking hilarious, mate! Did you see the way that fucking zombie's head blew up? It was like a goddamn watermelon!" Several voices laughed, and Max crouched down further. Max listened as the men spoke about what had been a recent raid and the occupants they had found within the store. Mockery and laughter continued, and Max knew they needed to get away. Leading Jay down to the other end of the alley, they crept away unseen. They stayed low and went a few streets over before hearing a gunshot ring out, echoing over the city. They hurried onwards away from the sound, constantly watching behind them.

After another night huddled up in another abandoned shop, Max was feeling antsy. For the first time since his infection, he had dreamed, and while he couldn't remember what the dreams had been about, he woke with a stronger sense of urgency to get to Clara. He quickly woke Jay and had them eat on the move, anticipating reaching the train before midday.

The rest of the morning, Max couldn't take his mind off Clara, and for once he was grateful for Jay's lack of need for conversation. His thoughts were turned inwards, and it was comforting to have Jay's nearby presence with no demands on him other than to lead the way.

Max's dreams of the night before plagued his mind, and tiny snips of images kept fluttering through his brain. It was little details, like that fuzzy robe she wore, and her beautiful skin. These were the impressions he clung to. In his dreams, however, she was in trouble, and he saw flashes of a cage, and her being surrounded by other infected. Of course, he knew these were only dreams, but he couldn't help but feel more anxious and went as fast as he possibly could.

Before leaving Sue's, Max had spent a lot of time looking over the map and the area directly around the train station. Judging by a few of the signs they had passed, he guessed they were getting very close.

"Jay, we almost at train. Understand?" Max stopped and looked at the boy. Jay gave no response but stared at Max with earnest. Max sighed but decided to try to explain anyways.

"We go train. Faster than walking. Get to Clara," his voice cracked, "and then we home."

Jay seemed to sense the sadness and urgency in Max's voice and smiled in understanding. Max nodded and grabbed Jay's hand, leading him towards where he expected the station to be. Sure enough, around the corner stood a building with the letters Max was looking for.

TRAIN

Grinning, he pulled Jay forward, keeping an eye out both ways for any sign of people. Seeing no one, he rushed them into the building.

As he walked in, the immediate scent of blood, smoke, and human flesh struck him. Even with his reduced smell it was almost overwhelming. Holding out his arm, they stood in the doorway, waiting and listening. Something had obviously happened here.

In front of them were rows of benches with several glass booths behind them. A hint of smoke came from a pile of garbage off to the side, but no flame was visible. Bodies, at least a dozen visible, littered the ground in the immediate area. A large clock hung above it all and *everywhere* was blood.

Max could hear Jay sniffing and kept him at his side while he thought about what to do next. Whatever occurred here hadn't been long ago and he noticed the bodies still had the smell of 'fresh' protein. The train wasn't at the station right now, but he knew it was only a matter of time. According to Sue, several ran these tracks, and all would at least take him the direction he needed to go. If he was lucky, the first one would be the one all the way to Vancouver, and Clara.

Having heard no sounds, Max released Jay, who immediately rushed forth and pounced on one of the bodies. A happy groan rose up in the boy's throat as he ripped and gnawed and chewed. While Jay was happy enough with anything that contained protein, and wouldn't attack those Max told him not to, he was still driven by basic instinct. That included his predilection towards fresh, human meat. While The Smell was still appealing to Max, the grisly scene in front of him inspired no hunger and he decided to use the time while Jay was distracted to look around.

Max wandered through the station taking in the details of the carnage, still on high alert with the scent of so much death around him. Several of the glass booths had blood on either side and a few also had bullet holes, some branching out like webs decorated with red and pink. Based on where the bodies were, it looked like two groups had met by accident. One side was obviously infected and based on the fact the uninfected were by the door, he guessed they had been hiding out here, not realizing it was a hub for human transportation.

He imagined the surprise of both parties.

Shock.

Screams.

Chaos.

Death.

He saw it all run through his mind and the realization that so much death could be caused by what was, at the core, just a big misunderstanding, was a painful one. *If only people realized what we went through after being infected,* Max thought. *Maybe they wouldn't be so quick to kill us. And obviously even the infected with less functions like Jay can learn at least a bit.*

Max wondered if things were different in Vancouver, and how Clara was faring. He still didn't know if she was infected, dead, or immune, and as much as he couldn't wait to find her, he was a bit afraid of what he might find. For the first time, a new worry about finally finding her occurred to him. What if she was alive and didn't trust him? What if he went all the way across the country and she couldn't accept him like this?

As much as the thought pained him, he knew there was no sense in dwelling on it. He turned towards the back of the station to see if anyone was hiding out in any of the offices or other closed doors.

Ten minutes later he had gone through the rest of the rooms and confirmed that nothing else was alive in the building. Evidence of some small nests, like the one he had seen in the store, were in several of the offices, indicating that he was correct; this had originally been an infected hiding place. The most horrifying discovery had been the corpse of a young boy in one of the offices. The boy was pale and had blood around his mouth, indicating he was infected, but it was a hole in the middle of his forehead that truly broke Max's heart. Even the young had no reprieve from the terror their kind instilled in people. He closed the door behind him, hanging his head low to his chest.

He went back to Jay, who had gorged and was now snoring loudly on one of the bloody benches, oblivious to the aura of sadness that hung over the building. With nothing else to do, Max took a seat and waited for their train to arrive.

CHAPTER 27

Rachel knew that once or twice a week the cage was left with absolute minimal guards for meetings and status updates with Wolfe. After the poor reception she received in the last of these meetings, Rachel figured her presence wouldn't be missed. This would be her best opportunity to free the infected with the least interruption. She knew after she released them time would be minimal to get away. Packing a bag, she took only what was necessary, ignoring things like food, assuming they could get that on the way. What was truly important, however, was her research.

Printing off reports wasn't an unusual practice for her team, who had known from the beginning that should their generators fail all their work would be lost. They had been systematically backing things up onto external drives as well as paper records so that it would never be gone should there ever be a need for it in the future. While they had yet to come up with a cure, the information contained a lot about the progression of the virus and the effects on the human brain. Rachel hoped that one day the rest of humanity would see what she did when looking at this research. That the so-called "zombies" were simply infected, brain damaged people who needed humanity's help.

Taking care to grab only what she could carry, Rachel informed her colleagues she would be attending the meeting, while also telling Wolfe's men that she would be working in the labs. With the small amount of stolen time, Rachel made her way down to the cage.

Specialist Johnson didn't mind being left out of the meeting to watch the cage and actually enjoyed the mindless solitude the zombies afforded him. After Captain Wolfe had taken over, he had lost all respect for the chain of command. Their previous leader, General Grant, had been a harsh man, but one with experience and a sense of right, even if that sense tended to be on the crueler side. Wolfe, however, was lacking in experience and was only in charge because the few superior officers between him and General Grant had died in the move to Canada. While Johnson had no care about the level of cruelty Wolfe displayed, he also had no respect for the man either. Sitting and babysitting a cage of zombies seemed preferable to listening to that asshole drone on about his so-called status updates.

Suddenly, the doors swung open as Doctor Samborski entered the room, a person Johnson was not expecting to see. He had never liked her self-righteous attitude and immediately scowled at her.

"Go to the meeting, Doctor," He growled out at her as she approached him. As she walked towards him, a swagger in her step, Johnson got suspicious. He knew that walk; it was the walk of a woman who wanted him. It was a look he never thought he'd see on her, regardless of the fact she was an attractive woman.

"What are you doing here?" he asked warily.

Smiling coyly at him, she responded, "I heard you were all alone down here. I've been meaning to get you by myself for a while now." She ran a finger down the front of his uniform before hooking it into his belt loop. Johnson smiled darkly. Even the good doctor couldn't refuse him.

"Is that how it is, doctor? Well, it would be my *pleasure* to come visit your quarters later tonight," he replied with a grin on his face.

Shaking her head, she took a step back.

"I've always liked an audience." She gestured to the cage before lifting her shirt over her head, leaving her only in a bra. Johnson's grin kicked up another notch. He put his gun down and made to go over to her before she held her hand up.

"Nuh uh, baby…turn around for a sec. I have a surprise for you."

Liking where this was going, he turned around. Rachel chuckled softly.

"You know, baby, you could have told me sooner," he began before hearing an ominous click. Before he could turn around, the cage was open, and its occupants spilled out into the room.

"What the fuck!" he yelled as he rushed to grab his weapon. Three of the infected were on top of him before he could raise it. He felt teeth bite into his throat and warmth cover him. He didn't get to say another word before everything went black.

When Clara watched Rachel enter the room, she immediately rallied her friends together and whispered for them to stay close. She didn't know what was about to happen but assumed this was the moment she was waiting for. As soon as the soldier had his back turned, Rachel had rushed over to the cage with the keys stolen from his belt and opened it. The less intelligent occupants immediately ran out and attacked the man who had acted as their captor.

Clara watched one of them rip out his throat and felt no remorse. She remembered his part in taking her, and in killing that other helpless female.

While Clara was not a monster, she also had a healthy sense of vengeance. As the last to come out of the cage, she, Three, and Seventeen approached Rachel, who was putting her shirt back on.

"Disgusting pig," Rachel spat in the now dead soldier's direction.

"Good act," Clara replied smartly, receiving a small smirk from Rachel in return. "Now what?"

CHAPTER 28

By the next day, Max was getting impatient and debating the wisdom of how long they should be waiting. He wanted to get on the road to see Clara, and every day spent waiting at the station was another day wasted.

A few infected had been seen wandering around outside, but other than that, it was completely quiet. Jay was content with all the 'food' to eat, though Max still hadn't partaken and had instead stuck to the cat food. While he still felt the logic of not feeling guilt for eating the dead, he wanted to be different than the rest. In a world where the infected were considered ferocious zombies, he wanted to prove it was possible for them to live peacefully alongside the uninfected. Even if he was only proving it to himself.

Max paced the platform, watching for signs of an incoming train. He had already chosen a spot where he and Jay would be able to hide and hopefully get on without being noticed. Their bags were tucked away for a quick escape, and now all they could do was wait.

Around noon on the second day, he was rewarded with a far off rumbling. Excited, he ran inside to find Jay, who quickly abandoned his latest meal and followed Max outside.

They took up their hiding spot and waited. A few minutes later they were rewarded with a loud whistle and bell indicating that the train was now approaching. Keeping their heads down, Max peered over the top of the boxes they crouched behind and watched the long train pull up to the station and slow. Before it had stopped completely, several men jumped off onto the platform and ran inside with guns raised.

Max didn't know it, but a group of immunes had taken control of the rail early on and had been using the 'keep on the move' concept to avoid the infected. At each scheduled stop they would slow enough to check for movement. If it looked clear, they would stop and a few would disembark, searching the area for supplies before moving on. Staying on the move was a method of survival, and an effective one at that.

Not wanting to get onto any of the first rail cars where he had seen people jump off, he signaled Jay to follow him and crawled in the other direction until they reached the end of the platform. Staying low, they moved down the tracks and looked for an easy entry point.

The men inside the station quickly realized what had happened and spent little time inside. Only a few moments after the train had stopped, the men were ready to board and get moving again. Anywhere with this much blood and destruction wasn't worth trying to raid.

A loud whistle and the rumble of the engines told Max he had run out of time to look for a suitable car. As the train started to slowly roll forward he saw a car a few down from where they were that had an opening and appeared to be a cargo section. Not hesitating, he grabbed Jay's hand and ran towards the entrance, pushing the boy forward, before pulling himself onboard just as the train started to pick up speed.

While they didn't yet know where they were going exactly, Max was thrilled to have successfully boarded the train. Before his excitement could build too much, his blood ran cold as he heard a voice address him.

"Who are you and what are you doing on our train?"

Jay turned towards the voice with interest, but not aggression. Max turned towards the dark end of the cabin and saw over a dozen infected men and women staring back at him. Shock paralyzed Max as he stared dumbly at the group in front of him. The man asked again, "Who are you? Are you one of slow ones? Can you speak?"

Max cleared his throat and finally got his wits about him to respond. "Yes. I am Max. This Jay. He not speak, understand bit though." The man nodded at this.

"Don't know real name, but you call me Guy."

Max greeted Guy and looked questioningly at the rest of the group around him, who all seemed to be eyeing them back with a touch of unease. Max assumed they had experienced similar ups and downs with their own kind and felt understanding of them not immediately accepting their presence.

Hoping to put their minds at ease, Max decided to introduce themselves further.

"We take train, go to Vancouver. Other side of country." Max pulled out the photo of him and Clara and passed it to Guy. "We go find Clara. Meet friend in city. She say take train."

Guy nodded and handed the photo back.

"Never meet others like me before who talk. All like Jay, or worse." The infected around him nodded in understanding. Guy, who was obviously the leader of this little group, clarified further. "Not as many like us, but some."

Max nodded in understanding, but before he could ask any questions, he watched as one of the infected in the group, a young girl probably in her early teens, approached Jay. They all watched with interest, including Jay, who stood unmoving as he watched her approach.

Standing only a foot away, she stared at Jay and reached a hand forward. Jay pulled back slightly at first and then waited to see what she would do. Smiling, she put a hand on his chest and cooed at him before reaching out her other hand and putting his in it. Jay smiled uneasily and looked at Max for what to do. He smiled and nodded, which encouraged Jay to let out a little whoop and squeeze the girl's hand. She immediately grinned and put her head on his shoulder.

"This Cassie. She found us after she bit. Doesn't speak either but understands and follows. Think she likes your friend." Guy chuckled a bit at his own understatement as the two infected teens continued to coo and paw at each other, effectively breaking the tension in the cab.

Guy turned to Max and gestured to a place to sit across from him. "So, you say friend tell you about train?"

Max smiled and settled in to tell his story.

Max and Guy ended up talking long into the evening, comparing notes and survival tips. Jay and his new admirer were cuddled up asleep, along with most of the others. Another woman among the infected, Sam, had done an excellent job of getting the ragged group to cooperate and managed to organize everyone with an efficiency that impressed Max. After Max had shared some of his cat food and showed the others how easy the little tabs were, things got considerably more friendly.

"So what else protein?" Guy asked, wanting to know more about safer food sources for his people.

"Animal," Max replied, thinking back to what Sue had said. "Little fish, tofu…."

"What Tofu?"

"Don't know," Max replied, "but has protein."

Guy frowned. "Think we stick to animal and cans. Tofu not sound like food."

"Can made with cat on them good," Max informed him. "Easy carry and open."

Pleased with the new information Max had brought, Guy decided to impart some of his own knowledge. "What hurt for them, not hurt for us," he told Max. "We not feel like before. Must also be careful of cold. We not feel it as much as *Them*."

Max looked at Guy curiously. He had guessed as much, and only had one question: "If they are *Them*, what are we?"

Guy looked back at Max sadly and shrugged. "We zombies."

CHAPTER 29

Most of the infected, having no comprehension of the idea of escape, immediately rushed the compound once the solitary soldier was gone. A few had stayed behind to eat, but most continued on in search of revenge and the ever-persistent smell of living humans that permeated the compound. One had approach Rachel briefly, but on receiving growls from both Clara and Three they backed off and went in search of easier prey. Nine sniffed at her a few times but followed the lead of his companions. And then they were five.

Rachel warned them all to be quiet before leading them through the heavy doors when a single gunshot rang out from somewhere ahead. The others had found at least one soldier, apparently. They rushed onwards, knowing the sound would attract others.

Before Rachel had come downstairs, she took a moment to close a few doors on her way, hoping that this would automatically divert most of the infected in the direction of the ongoing meeting and, therefore, the majority of the compound's soldiers. Pleased that it seemed to have worked, Rachel led their small party through one of the closed doors and towards their freedom.

Every so often she would stop and listen to far off echoes and was amazed at their luck. It wasn't until Rachel thought this that she turned a corner and bumped right into one of the few female soldiers in the compound, Private Morgan.

"What the fu…" Morgan started to shout as she unleashed a stray shot, startled by the group of zombies she was suddenly confronted with.

Clara growled as she recognized the soldier. Instinct took over, much as it had the first time Clara saw her, and she dove onto the woman, heedless of the weapon in her hand.

Morgan shrieked as Clara flattened her, flailing and scratching with all her might. Just as Clara was about to lean in to bite her neck, one more shot rang out and blood splattered onto her face.

Clara looked up in shock to see Three now holding Rachel's gun, pointing it down at Morgan's head. Blood and bits of skull ran down Clara's face and into her open mouth.

"Why!" Clara exclaimed, more annoyed than anything at Three's interruption. Three looked down at her and held out his hand to pull her up.

"No time. We go."

Rachel stood there looking down on Morgan's body, dumbstruck at what had just happened. She had no love for the cruel woman, but seeing death close up was something she didn't think she would ever become familiar with. It was because of her that a non-infected had died. She remembered the rest of her team were still in the compound, hopefully holed up in the locked laboratory, and right then vowed to come back for them, if she could. She took a deep breath and swallowed hard, and without another backwards glance, they raced down the hallway.

Luckily, they managed to make it to the garage without further incident, and the four infected passengers put their trust in Rachel to take them away from their captors. With no easy way to get into the garage ahead of time, Rachel had trusted the car keys would be near the vehicles and had made sure to keep a city map in the bag she brought. Other than that, the rest was left to fate.

They drove out into the early afternoon sun, intending to get as much distance between them and the base as possible. Rachel knew generally which direction Clara's house was but wanted to take a somewhat less direct route to get there, just to stay clear of the major streets. If anyone survived the attack within the base, which there was a very real chance they would follow when they realized it was her that unleashed them. Rachel wanted to ensure that if anyone came after them they wouldn't have an easy time determining where they were going.

"Everyone okay?" Rachel finally asked about ten minutes later, once her heart had slowed down slightly.

"Okay," Clara responded for all. Three stared out the window with disinterest and contempt, Seventeen with curiosity, and Nine was busy staring at his feet with fascination.

Satisfied with this, Rachel pressed on.

CHAPTER 30

The next few days went by relatively quickly and were among the most peaceful in Max's infected life. He had determined that they were in fact going to Vancouver, an incredibly fortunate turn of events for him. He felt as though his luck was changing and was feeling optimistic and happy for the first time in his new life. Soon, he would find Clara again. After that he wasn't sure, but knew Guy had plans in which they could potentially join.

"North from Vancouver," Guy told him, "lots of trees. Forest. Now we know we eat animals, we go north, away from Them."

It was a solid plan as far as Max could tell. His meetings with the uninfected had been both fortuitous as well as incredibly dangerous, but never uneventful. Max's priority was going to be to keep Clara safe and happy, but mostly safe. He wasn't prepared to let her out of his sight ever again. Sam, being the one who had suggested the trip out of Ontario, pored over maps with Max and showed him where they hoped to go. He wouldn't be going with them when they got off the train, but he told her if he was able he would come find them once he found Clara.

The weather stayed pleasant most of the trip and Max found himself spending hours with his legs hanging out the open cabin door, watching the beautiful country roll by him, often with the picture of him and Clara held tightly in his hand. He was amazed by the varying landscapes passing him by, and while he was glad that they had been able to use the train to move more quickly, a small part of him wished he had been able to cross this great country at a more leisurely pace. *Maybe one day*, he thought to himself, smiling.

A few moments later, Jay came to sit beside him, having finally untangled himself from Cassie, who was still making cutesy eyes at him from across the train car.

"How you, Jay?" Max asked.

Jay grunted in response and looked over at Cassie then back at Max, a bit of a helpless look on his face. He laughed. "Yes, she quite taken with you." Again, a grunt in response.

Max looked over the boy who had been his companion since the hotel. Even though Jay hadn't regained his ability to truly speak, he had become a real friend to Max.

"Thank you, Jay." Jay stared back, waiting for him to finish. "I say it before but can't say enough. You not have to come with me, but you did. Help me go find Clara. Thank you, for all." Jay grinned back at Max, obviously pleased with the thanks and the sentiment.

The two sat there for the rest of the afternoon, watching the country pass them by.

"When stops, will be hard to get off. *They* run train. Will kill if see you," Guy explained to him. "Whistle means soon, means jump. We all jump."

Max gulped as he watched the scenery rush past them. Observing the train from afar, it hadn't looked that fast, but the thought of jumping off it was daunting. He trusted Guy though. Even though they had only met a short time ago, he felt they were alike in many ways.

"When?" Max asked, wanting to ensure he and Jay were both ready.

"Today," Guy told him. "Don't know when, but today."

A few hours later, everyone was ready to go. Sam kept everyone busy and made sure they were all prepared, their belongings all piled up next to the door. There was an uneasy sort of silence aboard. Even Cassie had quieted down and stopped harassing Jay so much, though she still made a point to sit beside the boy. Jay seemed to not mind so much at this point and Max wondered how much he really knew about what was going on. As much as he had tried to explain it to him, he had no idea what was going to happen when the time came.

After a while, the tension seemed to wear off as the hours ticked by and a sort of complacent lull fell upon them. Small groups were chatting, eating some of Max's gifts of cat food, and generally acting normal again. Except for Max, who grew more and more uneasy the closer they got. *This was it,* he thought as he looked at the approaching horizon. *Somewhere out there is Clara.* It was just as he had this thought that a loud whistle sounded overhead.

Immediately everyone jumped to action with varying levels of quickness. Max and Guy stuck their heads out the door and looked down the line to see the station approaching, just a spot still in the distance but coming closer with every passing second. Without needing to say anything the two men pushed the heavy doors open the rest of the way on both sides.

"This is it!" Guy yelled over the loud wind. Everyone prepared themselves along the sides.

"Hold heads!" Max shouted.

One second passed. Two…
"GO!"

Anyone watching would have laughed at the comical sight. Zombies flailing and throwing themselves off of a moving train. In ones and twos, they all hurled themselves off the train. One managed to remain upright, running down the slight slope, but then quickly face planted from the momentum.

Several did in fact hold their heads with Sam leading the way, trying more of the tuck and roll technique. A small pile of bodies tangled together in their landing. A few had basically just tossed themselves, ending up sprawled on the ground.

Max was getting ready to jump when he noticed Jay's hesitation. Cassie had already jumped, being one of the ones who had sprawled, but Jay still seemed uneasy.

"Come Jay!" Max shouted, worried about the impending train station that was growing ever closer. Jay hesitated another moment before putting his trust in the man who had cared for him so far. Together they leapt from the car, Max doing a successful roll while Jay splatted down onto the ground, landing on his face.

As soon as he landed, Max jumped up and ran over to the boy to make sure he was okay. Blood poured from his face, causing Max to panic, until he saw that it seemed to be coming from Jay's nose. Meanwhile, Jay sat in the dirt making faces and trying to figure out what the warm stuff on his face was. He licked his lips a few times before giving Max and brilliant and bloody grin.

"Good. Stay here!" Max smiled back before heading over to the other groups who had jumped previously. He noticed a few people were all congregating in one area and immediately went in that direction.

As Max approached, he found that not all had made it off safely. One of the women, a non-talker, had broken her neck on impact. Cassie knelt over her, sobbing in the most pathetic way. Max wondered if it was her mother.

Sam murmured something in the prostrate girl's ear. Cassie continued to sniffle, but whatever Sam had told her made her cease wailing. Max noticed that Jay was heading over to the girl and hoped that he would be able to comfort her.

Everyone else other than the woman seemed to be okay. A few scrapes and bruises that weren't felt so much as seen. Jay seemed to be looking the worst with the blood from his nose covering his face and chest.

"Max okay?" Guy asked as he approached, receiving a nod in return. Max was about to reply further when another whistle was heard down the line and they saw the train come to a stop. Guy frowned a bit and told everyone to get together; they needed to move out of the open. Jay offered his hand out to Cassie and led the girl, following the rest of the group to the safety of the nearby forest.

Everyone regrouped in the forest, taking their time to splash water on their faces from a nearby stream. Compared to the cities that they had all just come from, the freshness and colors of the forest around them were breathtaking. Even though it was almost autumn, most of the trees around them remained green. A few were marked with yellows and oranges, the only indication of the impending season. The air smelled clean and everyone seemed to enjoy the quiet and peaceful change of scenery.

Max, however, started to get anxious again, wanting to get moving. He was so close to Clara now, but he also didn't know how to find her from here. Not knowing how long it would take, he didn't want to wait around. He glanced over at Jay, who was still comforting the girl. *Jay has done so much for me*, he thought. *We can wait a little longer.*

Settling down onto a fallen log, Max received a small nod and grateful smile from Guy. He immediately returned it and curled up to get a bit of rest before he continued on the rest of his journey.

Max woke up to a sky of pinks, oranges, and reds above him. For a moment, the ethereal beauty of it took his breath away and he could do nothing but stare. Birds around them seemed to have grown accustomed to their presence and were chirping away in the treetops, a peaceful sound that only added to the ambience.

Sitting up, Max noticed that the setting seemed to have affected everyone else as well—all except Cassie, who was currently curled up asleep with her head in Jay's lap. The boy seemed more content than ever before and Max was glad he decided to wait before leaving. Smiling at Jay, he got up and walked over to the end of the clearing, stretching and admiring the beautiful morning for one last moment.

Max was honestly amazed at how long he slept, but supposed his body felt comfortable enough in this place to sleep so deeply. He also took a moment to relieve himself, something he had figured out to do early on, more so because of the uncomfortable wetness and muscle memory than the actual feeling of need. He then washed his face in the stream. Once finished, he headed over to Guy, who had been watching him since he woke up.

"You leave?" Guy asked simply.

"Yes. Find Clara," Max reminded him. Guy nodded at this, but then gestured over to Jay.

"You want leave Jay? Make Cassie happy. Safe with us."

Max blanched a bit at the suggestion. Though he had at one point contemplated leaving Jay with Sue, he hadn't even considered since then that Jay would ever do anything but be with him and Clara. Max wasn't positive if Clara and he had children, but he didn't think so. He felt as though he would remember. But Jay...Max felt so close to the boy, and he thought of all the roles Jay had played.

Food. Teacher. Patient. Student. Friend...And yes, now he felt more like a son. Someone to protect and to care for. Could he leave Jay behind if that was truly what he wanted?

Max walked over to Jay, who watched him with a sort of passive curiosity.

"Jay," Max began, "I leave soon. Finish. Find Clara." Jay nodded and made as if to move Cassie from his lap before Max held up his hand, effectively halting his movement.

"Jay, you not have to come," he pushed on. "Cassie here. You safe here. You have helped me so much. But you can stay. If you want."

Jay's face darkened a bit, displaying a type of emotion Max hadn't seen on the boy since he died. With unexpected care and precision, Jay moved Cassie's head and placed it gently beside him so he could stand up. Max rose with him, unsure of what to make of Jay's unprecedented reaction.

"Max," Jay said, strong and clear, staring him straight in the eye. "Clara." Stunned, Max could only stare for a minute before finally comprehending the loyalty he was being shown. Tears of gratitude filled Max's eyes.

Before he could react, Guy walked over and handed them their backpacks, smiling lightly at the two of them.

"Good luck. You always have place with us."

CHAPTER 31

By evening, Wolfe was fairly sure none of the freed infected remained loose in the base. Another nine of his people had died in the attacks, a doctor was missing, and he was livid. Storming down to the office after completing the headcount, he wanted to confirm the exact numbers of zombies that they had captured previously and make sure they were all accounted for.

Throwing his door shut, he sat at his desk and went to open his drawer when he noticed one of the files wasn't where he had left it. Picking up the papers, he realized it was in fact one of the files he was looking for: the zombie profiles. In particular, it was the profile that belonged to the blonde woman who had stood up to him the night before.

Wolfe knew that, while some of the zombies were smart, they weren't smart enough to come in here and go through his files, much less read them.

He looked through the rest of the files and counted, noting there were four fewer zombies than they had originally captured. And one less doctor. *Samborski.*

The realization hit him. It had to be her. *But why would she bother looking through the files?* he wondered. She had way more direct information in her labs. As he scanned through, he noticed the soldiers had left addresses of where each one was picked up. Holding the blonde woman's file, he stood up and prepared for a morning departure. He wasn't letting them get away that easily.

By evening, Rachel was finally starting to breathe easy, confident they hadn't been followed. The random dash through the city had been effective.

They could make their way to Clara's in the morning, and she knew they weren't in an area they were likely to be found.

As they drove through the ruined city, she was overcome with horror and sadness at the state the world had become while she had been hiding out researching the virus.

Rachel knew the numbers, the probability of survival. Yet she hadn't seen the evidence of what was left behind. Coming up from Seattle she had been in a van with no windows and had been so afraid hearing some of the destruction of those around her that she hadn't paid attention during the journey. Seeing it now tore at her heart and soul in a visceral way that numbers on a piece of paper just couldn't compare to.

Several times there had been cars in their way that they needed to navigate around, which wasn't shocking. Her heart clenched when she saw people hunched over dead in their driver's seats, seeming to have died while on the move. The worst were the children, some of which had obviously turned on their drivers sometime before stopping. Rachel did her best to ignore the carnage.

Many people had ended up dying in their homes or in hospitals, and the entire city had the faint miasma of decay from the thousands upon thousands of corpses left rotting.

She wiped away the tears prickling her eyes and focused on the road ahead.

Clara was also very affected by the sight of the city, which she hadn't seen since her turning. Words drifted through her mind prompted by the visuals she was seeing.

House. Tree. Flower. Car. Fire. Body….

Distantly, she heard Rachel's voice inform everyone she was going to have them stop for the night. Although Clara wanted to keep moving, to find Max, she suddenly felt more tired than she could remember feeling since waking up in her home. *A few hours sleep*, she thought, *then home….*

They pulled up to a random warehouse that Rachel thought was probably a homeless haven, even before the virus hit. The glass windows were all long gone, and the copper oxide smell lingered in the air amid the ever-present smell of death. After Three went inside and declared it empty, they hid the car and entered to find a spot to rest. Once they went inside, Clara curled up in the corner and drifted off to the sounds of the others talking late into the night.

"We should name him Hudson," Max said as he rubbed her flat belly. Giggling, Clara asked how he knew it would be a boy.

In a mock display of upset Max scoffed, "Well, of course he's a boy! You think I could handle another little princess like you running around?"

"What do you mean by that!" she cried, playing along with his game. Max smiled at her. A smile that melted her heart and made her feel like the most important person in the world.

Leaning down to kiss her, he whispered, "Wake up, Clara."

Clara shot up, confused and bewildered. Looking around, she noticed everyone was asleep except Rachel, who was standing by the doorway keeping watch. Clara sat there a moment longer, trying to decipher what had just occurred.

Dream, she thought to herself. *That was a dream.*

She couldn't remember having dreamt before this, and wondered if it was truly a dream, or if it was a memory. She pressed her hand to her stomach. Did she and Max already have a child she had forgotten? She didn't think so, but it had felt so real it was hard to convince herself otherwise. She thought back to the empty room she had seen before being taken from her home, the small childlike animals lining the walls, and wondered if she had missed something in her haste to look for food.

Clara picked herself up off the ground and quietly made her way over to Rachel, careful not to disturb the others. She noted that Three was actually asleep and not watching over them as he usually did. She couldn't help but wonder if he felt safe with them, or just felt safe away from the soldiers.

Rachel didn't turn around as she approached, but Clara assumed she knew she was there.

After a moment's hesitation, Clara pressed forward. "Rachel?" she asked quietly.

The doctor turned to look at her. "Yes?"

Clara fiddled with her robe for a moment, unsure of how to ask the questions she wanted to know.

"I dream…" she began, making Rachel's eyes widen slightly, "I dream of Max. He sing to my belly, like baby in there."

Rachel nodded, prompting her to continue. "You do test. You tell if I have baby before?" She finished, looking up at Rachel with pleading eyes.

Although Rachel had answers, she had hoped when she first found them that it would never be something they discussed. "There was some scarring...inside you," she replied. "It indicates you may have had a difficult pregnancy before, but no, I don't think you've ever had a baby."

Nodding, Clara walked back to the corner in silence. For the rest of the night she remained awake, thoughts of Max and the pitter patter of little feet running through her mind. For the first time, she wasn't sure if she wanted to remember or not.

At sunrise, they were off.

CHAPTER 32

Once upon a time, Jay had taught Max to head west to find Clara. With nothing more than a few cans of cat food and the tire iron from so long ago, Max and Jay set out towards Vancouver to find her. Hoping he would recognize more along the way, Max simply used the advice that had started him on his path.

By the time the sun was high in the sky, Max was grinding his teeth at the slow pace with which they were moving. In comparison with the high-speed train they had just been on, this was just tedious. Deciding to see if he could figure out a car or something, they headed towards the nearby suburbs. Getting into the first residential area, Max indicated to Jay to keep quiet. With civilization also came many risks. Unfortunately, Jay's nose had been hurt worse than either of them anticipated during the jump, and a constant whistling now followed them. Max cringed but hoped at least the consistency of the whistling would be less noticeable than sudden noises. Max heard vague noises a few times in the distance, but never anything close enough to be of major concern.

As they snuck around, Max couldn't help but get a sense of familiarity from the area and the vibe of the houses surrounding them. Vague memories of his home came back to him, more as feelings than specific images.

After a while, Max noticed a house with the door open but a closed garage and decided to try and see what was there. He hoped the open door meant the residents had left. Once they got to the front door, Max leaned forward and smelled the air, but didn't notice any strong scent of the living, blood, or decay. Unlike Sue's shop, there were fewer signs of carnage and more just general mess and a feeling of something rushed remaining. They were in the clear.

Wandering into the house, Max searched for a few moments while Jay fiddled with what had once been a child's toy before Max found the inside door to the garage. Max called Jay over but was disappointed when they opened the door to find it empty.

Just as Max was about to turn to find another house, Jay stepped past him and wandered into the garage over to a bike with some contraption attached to the back.

"Mmmmmm," Jay moaned happily as he lovingly caressed the bike before looking up at Max hopefully.

"We try that already, Jay, but you fall…" Max stopped as he realized what was attached to the back of the bike. *This could work.*

For the rest of the day, Max and Jay rode openly down the streets towards Vancouver without a single fear of the uninfected. With some extra clothes liberated from another nearby house, they had covered most of their pale skin and their bloody clothing. They then put on baseball hats to hide their faces. The small bike trailer attached to the sturdy bike just barely fit Jay, and Max was rewarded with a bit of extra stability in riding the two of them. As long as they stayed on the road, Max didn't tire easily and just needed to focus on his feet.

Having made decent progress, Max stopped them for the night as the sky started to fade to purple. They found a shed on the edge of what looked to be a deserted property and got ready to settle in for the night. Max was starting to see signs with the symbols and letters he knew meant Vancouver, and more specifically the city he knew he lived in, Surrey, and hoped he would recognize more by the following day. Rewarding them both with an extra can of food, they drifted off to the sound of Jay's whistling nose.

In the middle of the night, sounds of struggle woke Max. In the darkness of the shed, it was difficult to discern what he was seeing, but it looked like an infected woman was attacking Jay!

Springing into action, Max jumped up and grabbed the back of the woman's shirt, effectively tearing her off Jay. The flimsy door crashed underneath her as Jay struggled to get up from his own tangle of limbs. She immediately jumped up and growled at Max, preparing to strike again. Max stood in front of Jay and growled as a gust of wind blew the baseball hat off his head.

The woman immediately paused, taking note of his alabaster skin that seemed to glow in the moonlight. Max noted the change and realized that she thought they were uninfected. Her nose was obviously broken at some point based on the angle and the blood on her face, and Max wondered if it had affected her sense of smell. For a moment, they only stared at each other. He maintained his defensive stance but didn't really feel she was a threat any longer. After a few minutes, he finally told her, "Go." The woman scampered off around the side of the shed and out of sight.

They had no further disturbances for the rest of the night.

The next day, Max brought them onto the highway, and within a few hours was rewarded with more familiarity. With no vehicles moving on the road, Max only had to navigate through a few crash zones where cars littered the streets. He noted the lack of life but assumed streets with no cover anywhere weren't appealing to anyone, infected or otherwise.

The reassurance of the recognizable landscape encouraged Max even more and he pushed hard until he saw an exit sign whose symbols were like alarm bells in his head.

City of Surrey.

Max knew where they were. Taking the exit, Max raced towards his home. And, he hoped, to Clara.

Wolfe and eleven of his most ruthless men rushed towards the destination that had been left for them. By the time everything had been organized, there would have been no way to track them down if he hadn't noticed the folders out of place. Wolfe was betting that he was right and looked forward to bringing the doctor back to the General at the base, who hadn't been released from the separate containment unit in the chaos of the breakout. Only a select few knew about that or had access. While General Grant had died, he was very much awake again. And he was very much hungry, and angry. Wolfe couldn't wait to introduce the doc to his special specimen.

"Move it!" he shouted as he grinned. It was going to be a good day.

Clara got out of the car and stared up at the familiar house. She remembered what waking up had felt like, that awful feeling of uncertainty and confusion. She remembered walking through the house and feeling lost.

But now, she looked up at the house and remembered Max.

Home.

Unable to wait any longer, Clara awkwardly ran towards the house, her stained robe trailing behind her.

She ran inside and noted the furniture strewn about, destroyed, and realized it hadn't been like that before. *Had Max been here?*

"Max!" she cried, rushing up the stairs, pushing her body past its comfortable speed. Throwing open the bedroom door she was rewarded with nothing more than a stained bed and a considerable number of flies and other bugs.

Not letting this deter her, Clara ran through the rest of the house, calling for Max the entire time. She took an extra moment to pause in front of the unfinished, empty bedroom but moved on, focused on finding Max.

Meanwhile, Three, Rachel, and Seventeen had exited the car and made their way to the front door with Nine trailing slightly behind. They watched her with pity in their eyes as she desperately searched.

On her second pass through the house, she stopped in the kitchen and Clara finally let her shoulders slump. Gripping the counter, she closed her eyes and tried not to let her body shake. She heard someone walk into the room but didn't look up. A moment later, Three's arms wrapped around her and Clara let herself fall into the old man's embrace. She found herself, not for the first time, grateful for his comfort and presence. Silent tears ran down her face.

Max wasn't here.

"You be okay," Three told her. "We here with you."

Clara started to nod before bursting into heavy sobs. Three said nothing more, silently rubbing her back.

After a moment, they heard noises coming from the front and Rachel's voice rang out with urgency, calling Clara to the door.

Rushing over, Clara and Three looked to see what she was yelling about. All of a sudden, big arms enveloped Clara in such a hug she couldn't even see who they belonged to.

A familiar smell filled Clara's nose and fresh tears sprang to her eyes.

"Max."

"Clara," Max sobbed, holding his wife tightly. The world seemed to drop away as they held one another.

Despite everything they had been through, they found each other.

After a moment, Max recalled the others around them, including a brown-haired woman whom he suspected was uninfected. Max didn't care in the slightest, though. In that moment, as he held Clara tightly against him, he felt nothing but gratitude and love.

Placing her face into his hands, Max looked deeply into her face and was rewarded by a pair of familiar and stunning blue eyes looking back at him. All his fears of her not accepting him, or of her being dead, faded away when he looked into her eyes and saw nothing but acceptance and love.

"Love you," she whispered up at him, causing him to lean down and kiss her passionately.

A small whoop coming from the pale brown infected woman behind him interrupted their moment. An older man poked the woman to shush her, but she only snickered.

"Hi, Max," the woman said, giving him a little wave and a knowing grin. "Clara, huh? Better than Seventeen." She wagged her eyebrows a bit and winked.

Clara laughed at this. She was so overwhelmed with seeing Max again that she hadn't even realized she now knew her real name. Max looked at Seventeen and then to Clara for an explanation.

"Max, this Seventeen, Nine, and Three." Max nodded, pleased that Clara hadn't been alone, though he could tell she had obviously been through the sickness. He held her a bit tighter, thinking of what Jay had gone through in the hotel and the vague memories of his own death. He felt guilty he hadn't been there for her like he should have been. Remembering the uninfected woman, Max turned around for an explanation and introduction.

"I'm Rachel," she introduced herself. "I'm a doctor. I won't hurt any of you. I helped get them here. Clara's been looking forward to this for quite some time." She smiled warmly.

Jay, having finally untangled himself from the trailer on the bike in which Max had left him, wandered over at this opportune moment. Ignoring everyone else, he walked right up to Clara. Max smiled, guessing that Jay remembered her from the many times Max had been holding her picture.

"This is Jay. Jay, this…" Max began, before being interrupted with one of the only words Jay had said since his turning. "Clara." Max grinned widely, placing a hand on Jay's shoulder.

Just as Clara was about to greet the boy, a gunshot rang out hitting the door beside them.

CHAPTER 33

Several things happened all at once.

Max threw himself over Clara. Everyone else standing in the doorway immediately dropped to the ground and looked for the source of the shot that was fired. A voice rang out over the yard.

"Don't move! I'd rather you come alive, but I'm happy to take you fuckers dead too!" Wolfe shouted, a dozen men around him all aiming their weapons at the small crowd. Max felt Clara flinch under him at the sound of the man's voice. A deep growl grew in his throat at the thought that this meatbag scared his wife, his Clara.

"Doctor, really?" Wolfe mocked from across the lawn. "Betraying your own kind for some fucking zombies?"

Rachel glared at him. "They're fucking people, you monster!" Behind her, the infected all bared their teeth.

Wolfe began laughing, but quickly stopped as a few faint but distinct moans carried in the breeze. Looking around, Max noticed other infected coming out of various houses and other hiding spots in the vicinity. Apparently, the loud echo of the gunshot had brought them out, a dinner bell for the infected. Multiple small groups from the area slowly shuffled towards them. It wasn't long before Wolfe's men had a lot more targets.

"Shoot!" The command rang out over the area.

Max and everyone else in the door quickly pushed themselves inside. Unfortunately, the earlier warning shot had hit the hinge of the door, rendering it unable to close. They all stood inside the doorway watching as their infected brethren descended upon the soldiers. Max noticed the doctor fussing over Clara, who was waving her away, but quickly turned his attention back to the scene outside.

More and more infected poured out from the houses and alleys, making their way towards the loud and tantalizing men in the middle of the street, who were now seriously outnumbered. Down the street and out of range, he saw a few groups huddled together talking. *Guy was right*, he thought, *there are more like us*. His heart jumped into his throat as he watched one trio break away and make their way towards the soldiers.

Max looked at the men in the street, their eyes filled with hate as they shot at anything within range. Some of the infected approaching were slower, and he saw one soldier let a young infected man approach only to pull out a cattle prod and zap him. The soldiers laughed as the boy's body danced to the current, bleeding and burning on the ground in front of him. All the while the infected youth screamed.

The dam of fury and outrage in Max burst as he listened to the screams. Before anyone could stop him, he rushed forward into the center of the yard and shouted as loud as he could.

"LISTEN! EVERYONE PLEASE STOP! LISTEN!"

In front of him, the group of soldiers stopped shooting, in shock rather than recognition of what he had said. Most of them had never heard a zombie speak before, not having believed Rachel's speech. They stared open-mouthed as Max stood there with his arms raised.

The infected that were not smart enough to speak recognized another of their own and stopped momentarily, imitating those around them who were watching Max. Clara struggled to get out to him but was held in place by Three, who seemed to accept, if not understand, what Max was doing. The only sound on the block was Clara's voice calling out for Max and the ever-present whistling of Jay's nose.

Max realized that he had everyone's attention, and if he had still been able to blush, he would have reddened considerably. But not wanting to lose momentum, he attempted to get out what he needed to say.

"We are all people." He paused for effect, looking between the soldiers and the infected. "We not need hurt each other. You that are like me, there is much other food. I teach and help you. We not all talk, not all smart. But we help each other." Max stopped and looked over at the uninfected men who were looking at him with expressions ranging from awe to anger. "If you just not hurt us anymore, we all be friends. Live…"

A single shot ran out, breaking the carry of Max's voice with a loud bang. He didn't feel the pain but felt the impact and saw the blood that rushed from his shoulder. Max fell to the ground as Clara escaped Three's grasp.

The scene around them turned back to chaos.

Clara ran forward towards Max, heedless of the battle that was once again commencing around them. Many of the soldiers were still stunned and the smarter infected took the moment of surprise to attack. Clara had eyes only for Max.

"Max," she sobbed as she reached him, throwing herself down beside him. More blood covered her already filthy robe as she brought her forehead down to his, her tears pouring down both of their faces.

"I okay, Clara," Max whispered as he tried to sit up. Clara attempted to support his back to help him up when suddenly Jay was at their side helping her. She noted that the bleeding had already slowed and the wound was not as serious as she had first thought. The two of them helped Max stand, and Clara was pleased to see that their new infected 'friends' had caused quite the distraction. Glad for the respite, Clara put her arm under Max and started walking him back to the house, intent on getting them to safety. Jay straggled along beside them, slightly distracted by the carnage all around. Several of the soldiers had branched off towards their targets and small skirmishes went on all down the street.

Just as they were about to cross the threshold, a familiar laugh made Clara pause.

"Not getting away that easy," Wolfe gloated from behind them, his pistol pointing in their direction. Max and Clara tensed, holding one another and waiting. A low growl came from Clara's throat as she glared at Wolfe. The captain squinted as he glared straight back.

"You've been a pain in my ass since we picked you up," he stated, aiming the gun at her. With unprecedented quickness, Jay rushed forward to defend them and a single shot rang out around them.

For a moment, time stood still as they watched Jay fall, blood pouring from his chest.

Something in Max snapped.

A guttural and raw sound ripped from Max's throat.

All previous guilt and thoughts of humanity dissolved as he roared and rabidly attacked the man who had shot Jay. Before the man could aim again, Max was on him, knocking the gun out of his hand and tackling him to the grass. For a moment the two men grappled, Max's moment of surprise losing its effect as his less responsive limbs tried to fight him off.

Max's shoulder began to bleed in earnest as both men struggled to get the upper hand. Max quickly realized this wasn't going to end in his favor as the man hit him once, and then again in the face. The third time, Max opened his mouth instead and bit deeply into the man's forearm, eliciting a scream that was like music to his ears. He ripped the chunk off as he dove for the man's face.

Trying to defend himself, Wolfe turned his head allowing Max to latch onto his neck, his teeth gnashing through skin and muscle as he ripped out the man's throat. Blood covered him, and he roared at his own victory as the man went limp under him. With glee, he chewed through the flesh, his first true taste of fresh human meat. His chest heaving, he looked up to see

Seventeen and Three rush past him, pouncing on the remaining soldiers. Screams echoed over the lawn, but this time they meant nothing to Max.

Getting up, Max looked behind him at Clara, who was holding Jay in her arms, tears running down her face. Rushing over to her side, he knelt and took Jay into his own arms, heedless of the blood coating his body. *After all we've been through....* His chest seemed to tighten, squeezing the breath out of him.

"Max," Jay whispered, giving him a small smile. Max squeezed his eyes shut and brought the boy to his chest as he took his final breath.

"Thank you for saving her," Max whispered back as he broke down right there on his own doorstep. Bloody and beaten, he sobbed as Clara wrapped her arms around them both.

CHAPTER 34

It wasn't long after that they noticed the guns were no longer firing and looked up to see the last few soldiers retreating. The sight of their captain's throat being ripped out had been the last straw. A few of the mindless infected remained, feeding on the corpses left behind. Rachel had come out to try to help Jay, but by then it was already too late.

Clara watched Max and could see the wheels turning in his head. The deep furrows in his brow and the darkness in his eyes spoke of loss and defeat. Doing the only thing she could think of, she stood by him, gripping his hand tightly, hoping he knew she was there for him. He smiled down at her, a sad smile, but one that made her heart sing nonetheless.

Max, she thought to herself. *And I am Clara. It will all be okay now....*

While Max was doing his best to put on a brave face for Clara, he felt lost. He had done what he set out to do in finding Clara only to lose Jay. The injustice of a world so prejudiced against them grated on Max's soul and he wondered if there was more he could have done.

Three and Seventeen made their way back over with a few new friends in tow. Max was too distracted to be excited about the idea that there were more people like them. Like Jay. He hardly paid attention as one man walked right up to him and extended his hand in a greeting Max had almost forgotten.

"Good kill," the man stated, nodding at him.

Max knew better. It hadn't been a good idea to kill that man. He knew that this wasn't the way for people like them to be accepted, but Max didn't have it in him to argue. He finished shaking the man's hand and stepped towards Three.

"Max," Three said nodding towards Seventeen and the others behind him, "we not stay here. Go find new home together. You come?"

Max stared at the group in front of him for a moment as he considered this. More than ten men and woman stood in front of him, pale and infected, the same as them. Around them, others feasted on the bodies of the fallen. Max squeezed Clara's hand and without a word he turned around and walked into his house.

They all watched him go and he heard Three's voice behind him. "No, let him go. Give time."

Max was grateful for the man's understanding. He did need a moment.

He wandered through the once familiar house holding his injured shoulder, a small trail of blood drops following behind him. All around were pictures of him and Clara, small knick-knacks that triggered insignificant memories of times past.

He stopped in their bedroom, taking note of the ruined bed that looked so much like the one he and Jay had left behind in the hotel room. His heart clenched a moment.

Max considered how much he had wanted his memories back when he first woke up but was coming to realize that, no matter how much of his former self he regained, things would never be the same.

He looked down to where a rogue picture lay at his feet. Leaning over to pick it up, he his heart clenched looking at the lovely picture of his wife. *Things would never be the same*, he thought, *but they can still be good.*

He thought of everything that happened and of their new friends. Despite his gratitude for all they had done, he knew that he couldn't protect Clara as effectively with them. Not in this world.

With a new sense of resolve, he walked back to the front of the house.

"No," Max said. "Thank you for taking care of Clara. But we go. Clara and me."

Seventeen opened her mouth to object, but before she could speak Three gave her a meaningful look and shook his head. A moment later, Three turned back to them and nodded.

The doctor stepped forward from inside the house and cleared her throat. "Does anyone need a ride anywhere? I need to go back to the base. With Wolfe gone, there are things I need to do, to find out. But I can help first."

That evening, they buried Jay under a tree in their backyard. Max wanted to speak, to say something, but the words caught in his throat. Rachel saw his difficulty and asked if he minded, and surprised them all with a beautiful, clear soprano version of '*Yesterday.*' Max watched the tears fall from Clara's face despite having just met Jay, and he wondered where his own were. He thought perhaps she was crying the tears he couldn't.

While Clara and many of the others slept, Max talked with Three and another man, who called himself Bino. Max had asked, and the man told him when he woke up someone had asked him if he was "albino" because of his light skin, and he decided he liked it.

"They captured many of us," Three muttered to the others. "We were moved from places. By *Them*."

Bino cut in, "You mean the HOs?"

"What are hoes?" Three asked.

"Healthy ones."

"Yes, Them. The HOs."

The men nodded solemnly at each other.

Max sat silently, absently listening to them talk, but actually deep in thought.

"Max," Three asked, causing him to look up at the older man, "tell us about your journey." Bino nodded in agreement, and Max sighed.

"Well, first there was this fucking doorknob…."

After relaying his story to Three, Bino, and a few other stragglers, Three told him a bit of what they had been through, what Clara had been through. The thought of anyone hurting his beautiful wife or keeping her in a cage infuriated him and he pardoned himself from the small gathering.

Entering the house, he stood in the kitchen for several moments to calm himself. His violent reaction at Wolfe was uncharacteristic, and while he didn't really regret it, the rage he felt now scared him. There were few things that could truly anger Max and, as with most people, anyone hurting someone he loved was a hard limit. As he calmed himself, he heard a slight rustling coming from the other room. He knew Clara was upstairs asleep with Seventeen and a few others.

Turning into the living room, he found the doctor, Rachel, sitting at the table looking through some folders she had spread out over their dining room table. She was so entranced with what was in front of her she didn't notice Max approach.

"Hello."

"Holy shit!" Rachel exclaimed, clutching her chest. "You scared the crap out of me, Max!" She chuckled a bit at her own reaction, which elicited a small smile from Max.

"Okay I sit?" He asked her, pulling up a chair on her nod of approval. Turning her attention to him, she subtly took in his details and features. The picture Clara had shown her was quite obviously the man in front of her, but there was a melancholy aura about him that she didn't think was entirely due to the effects of the virus, or even the death of his friend.

"So, Max," Rachel started, not entirely sure what to say to the man before her, "how are you doing with everything?" Max shrugged a bit as he thought of how to respond.

"I…okay. Was a lot today. But glad Clara is here, safe." He cleared his throat before continuing. "Thank you. For helping Clara and others. Not all people nice to '*zombies*'." He spat the last word. Rachel frowned slightly, wondering what types of people he had encountered on what she now knew was a cross country adventure for him.

"It was my pleasure," she responded honestly. "I found out quite a bit about the virus while studying it, about people who were infected like you. I tried to get others to understand and help." She sighed and gave a sad smile. "Unfortunately, it didn't really work, and now here we are."

"You tell me more?" Max asked, excitement and curiosity evident in his voice.

"Of course I will. What do you want to know?"

Late into the night, Rachel told Max all she knew about the virus. She did her best to explain how the virus affected people and what they could expect in the coming months. Not knowing if Clara had told him about the baby, she didn't mention it.

The next morning, Clara said her farewells to Seventeen, Three and the rest. It was bittersweet saying goodbye, and while she would never regret her decision to follow Max, she would miss them more than she expected. Rachel had helped her too, but in their captivity she had grown to rely on her numbered friends and was sad to see them go. As she hugged Seventeen, she looked over the woman's shoulder and saw Max standing there, smiling at her. A small, sad smile, but a smile nonetheless. He wandered off into the house and left Clara to her goodbyes. Three and Seventeen would go with the others that had been hiding in the area. They all had plans to join up with a bigger group. Max provided the maps given to him by Sam, knowing that she and Guy would welcome them with open arms. Rachel planned to go back to the compound to see what was left and help her colleagues who she thought remained.

Clara would always be grateful for everything they had done for her, but if Max wanted just her, then that is what she would do. The two of them were all that mattered. At least for now. Clara waved goodbye to all of her new friends, allowing herself a few tears before going to look for Max.

She walked through the house and found Max kneeling in the backyard, staring absently at the tree under which Jay was buried. She walked up to him and held him against her, kissing the curls on top of his head. He smiled up at her, and although she didn't know what would happen to them, she felt hope for the first time since she woke up. Smiling back down at him, she took his hand and gently placed it on her belly.

"One more thing, Max."

EPILOGUE

The sun is setting over our secluded forest home as I walk up behind my very pregnant wife and wrap my arms around her, or as far around as they will reach, anyway. Her beauty grows with every day and it's almost overwhelming to look at her. She smiles as she relaxes back into my arms and hums lightly, a noise so low in her chest that I feel more than hear it.

It has been almost eight months since we left Vancouver and headed north, just the two of us. Soon to be three. I think about Jay often, wishing it was four. Shortly after we arrived in our new home, I made a gravestone of sorts for him. Clara never questions me when I walk over the ridge and sit by it.

Over the past months, both of us have gotten better at speaking, at remembering. There are still many parts of our past life we forget, but it has become a bit of a game for us to remind each other of things the other has forgotten. During our long walk into the forest it was me who remembered losing the baby before FIRE. That is one thing I never reminded Clara of. Maybe she knows, but I won't bring it up. At times I feel guilty for keeping something from her, but the last thing I ever want to do is worry her. It's amazing how much losing your memory can erase so many sins of the past.

Under my hand I feel a kick and kneel to kiss it, making Clara giggle. That noise is the best sound in the world to me and I can't wait to make our baby giggle like that every day.

Once upon a time I felt helpless, unable to control the world around me. Unable to protect and care for those I love. History tells me I won't always be successful at this; however, it is moments like these that I remember why it will always be worth fighting for.

I have died and risen again. I have crossed an entire country and survived against all odds. I am strong, and I am a survivor.

THE END

EXCERPT
DEAD AWARE: VAGRANT YOUTH
CHAPTER 1

Typically, in September, Abby and her small band of misfits would be working to better secure their home for the impending cold season. For being a group of homeless youth, they made out pretty well with their decrepit home and had long ago learned tricks to ensure their home was as comfortable, warm, and dry as possible during the winter. This year, however, they had a new problem.

"Ike, I'm over here," Abby whispered loudly from across the alley. Ike quickly made his way across to Abby where they both froze, keeping their eyes wide for signs of danger. "Did you find anything?" He whispered back, keeping his gaze out on the streets. She shook her head. "Shit," he muttered, "We need a new system. The kid's gotta eat, and no one is throwing shit away anymore. No one's even outside anymore."

Abby sighed and nodded. For the past two years, she and Ike had become the unofficial leaders of a small group of homeless youth in Vancouver. Being the oldest, they had taken it upon themselves to ensure the welfare of the ones who couldn't care for themselves and to make sure that everyone contributed to their 'family.' One of the many jobs was dumpster diving to look for food, clothes or other useful items thrown away by the more fortunate.

Since the FIRE virus hit the city almost a week before though, this was no longer an option, and the household had run out of food almost two days ago. Being in an abandoned house without internet or phones, they hadn't heard all the details of the virus but from the bits they had heard they knew that it had taken the world by surprise and had a high fatality rate. Fearful for their small family, Abby and Ike had everyone stay inside, hoping to wait until it passed.

The only reason they ventured out of the house today was Joshua's complaining earlier of his stomach hurting, prompting Ike and Abby to go out looking to see what they could find to eat and find out about what was happening.

As soon as Ike and Abby had gotten into the city, they knew this was more than just a normal virus. The usually bustling streets of the city were almost totally devoid of life. A few cars were on the road but not many and all the shops and businesses were closed. As they walked down the street, an ominous presence seemed to hang in the air making them both feel uneasy.

"Abs, what should we do?" Abby thought for a moment. *Okay so dumpster diving is out, the few places that sometimes offer us old food are out, and even the stores are closed so we can't panhandle...*

"Abs?"

"Just give me a minute!" She snapped back, at once regretting her harsh tone when she saw the look on Ike's face.

"Sorry, man, I'm just stressed."

Ike gave her a small smile. "I get it Abs, don't worry." Ike looked around before he focused on a point in the distance, his eyes growing wide. "Hey, I got an idea! Why don't we head to the lake? If we go back and grab our bikes, it won't take too long, and we can maybe catch a few fish!"

Abby perked up slightly. She knew they had an old rod somewhere in the garage of the house and Ike was right, their bikes would get them there quickly.

"Okay. Let's do it!"

An hour later they had grabbed the bikes and were back on the road, this time on wheels. While the streets still seemed unusually quiet, having the wind blowing through their hair brightened their moods. It was early September, and the weather was still warm, with only that slight chill at night betraying the impending seasonal change.

When they were only a few minutes away from the water, loud shouts and the twinkling of broken glass could be heard up ahead. Instinctively, they both got off their bikes and crept quietly along the sidewalk towards the sounds of chaos. Being on the street for so many years, they both knew how to approach what sounded like a violent situation—being careful and undetected.

"Oh shit," Abby muttered as they peered around the corner. Up ahead was a grocery store, all of its front windows shattered. Inside, they could hear a group of people making the noise they heard from around the block. Abby tilted her head to the right, and the two carefully, snuck down a nearby alley where they could still keep watch, but also remain hidden.

Whoops and hollers could be heard from inside the mutilated store. A few minutes later, half a dozen men barreled out with shopping carts loaded with food and other stolen goods. Abby noticed an entire cart dedicated to liquor. Her eyes narrowed at the sight. *Because that is what is important during a viral outbreak... idiots...* The men talked loudly as they passed.

Staying out of sight, Abby and Ike waited for the group to leave. Even after the sounds of them fleeing were long gone, they both waited. Finally, Ike turned to Abby.

"We may as well go in, Abs," he stated, "The windows are already busted, and this will be a lot quicker than fishing."

Despite her hesitation to be *one of those street kids*, she quickly agreed. Things were worse than they thought if people were looting stores.

Leaving their bikes, they quickly and quietly made their way over to the storefront, peeking inside before entering. Inside they saw many of the sales racks were overturned and they could see the men had tried to get into at least one of the cash registers.

"Assholes not content to just steal; they had to wreck the place too, huh." Abby muttered under her breath, unimpressed with what she saw.

Although Abby had been homeless for almost three years now, she did her utmost to set an example for other people in her situation. She had been raised to be respectful and with morals in a well-off family. Her mother was Afghani, her father Canadian and Abby had a stunning combination of their features. With thick dark hair and lashes, flawless skin and a brilliant smile, she was a beautiful girl. That combined with a fierce intelligence and quick wit, she attracted friends, and suitors, with ease. Her one mistake and biggest regret had been getting involved with a man in his thirties when she was barely sixteen. Less than a year later she was on the streets, escaping the wannabe pimp.

Thinking her family would never take her back, she roamed the streets by herself for months before coming across Ike. She found him selling himself on Hastings, a well-known area for junkies and whores. Intrigued by the way he held himself and his grown out mohawk, she introduced herself and after one conversation, she felt a kindred spirit. The two of them ended up befriending more young misfits and thus, their family was born.

Abby didn't steal, do drugs or sell herself, and she expected the other members of her small family to follow her example. They shared everything and worked together, and, in all honesty, they were well off considering their situation.

Abby despised the idea of stealing, but the urge to care for her family and make sure they were fed, was stronger. The few hours they had been out today had been enough to show her that FIRE was more than they had initially thought, and she knew she needed to swallow her pride and stock up on supplies if she was going to keep everyone alive.

"I think it's clear," Ike whispered. Abby nodded. Careful of the shards of glass, they made their way into the store. They quickly filled both their backpacks and grabbed several more bags of nonperishable food, some batteries and a couple of sleeping bags. Their combined years of experience on the streets made it easy to prioritize what they knew they would need most, and within fifteen minutes they were back on their bikes rushing home with backpacks on each of their fronts and backs and bags tied to the backs of their bikes.

"What the hell was with that, huh?" Ike asked Abby as they rode.

"I guess it's worse than we thought," she responded before noticing a newspaper fluttering across the road. *Maybe the paper will have some info. Man, I miss having a cell some days.* Wobbling under the weight of the bags, she stopped her bike and ran over to grab a clean copy from a nearby stand. Ike nodded with approval, grabbing the paper and stuffing it into one of the bags as Abby got back on her bike before they continued on.

While going through a more residential section of the city, they heard a loud wail coming from ahead. Screeching their bikes to a stop, they watched as a few houses up a woman and man fought loudly. The exact words indistinct due to how far away they were, Abby couldn't help but think that the woman was pleading, sorrow and anger mixed in the tone of her voice.

Walking their bikes across the street they both did their best to remain inconspicuous but were curious about the scene in front of them.

As they got closer, they realized the man and woman were fighting over a body!

They spoke in an unfamiliar language, but it was obvious the man was trying to take it out of the house and the wailing woman was protesting. Almost parallel to the house, Abby and Ike finally got a better view of the commotion before them. No wonder the woman was so distraught; the body was that of a child, a child who couldn't have been more than ten. The woman's cries pierced both of their hearts, and Abby quickly blinked the tears away before they could blind her. As quickly as they could, they moved on, even more intent on getting home.

When they finally reached their house, relief washed over them both. It had been a stressful day, and both were grateful they wouldn't have to go out for a while. Neither of them told the others about the dead boy.

Get your copy of Dead Aware: Vagrant Youth on Amazon and Kindle!

AUTHOR'S NOTE

Thank you so much for reading and I hope you enjoyed!

If you enjoyed this (and hey, even if not!) **please leave a review**! Independent authors such as I rely on your reviews to ensure our stories reach as many people as possible. Reviews are the #1 way you can support an independent author (though we also accept hugs and alcohol).

A Zombie Journey is a story I have had in my head for about fifteen years, and in 2019 I set off to write the story of two zombies crossing the country to find one another. Obviously, the idea developed from there and turned into the story you just read. At times, Max and Clara had their own ideas of how they wanted their story to go.

I also want to apologize to my readers and poor Max for Jay's untimely death. Honestly, it wasn't planned initially and just happened. It hurt me deeply and was something I tried to 'write out,' but ultimately, it is what needed to happen in this story (though I have considered writing a story of Jay pre-FIRE, including his week before meeting Max, so would love to hear interest levels on this!).

Lots more in the Dead Aware world to come, including *Dead Aware 2* (Release date TBD but will be in 2019), picking up Max and Clara's story. Will they have a 'zombie' baby? Will they join up with Guy and the others? Will people finally accept the infected and live together in harmony? What I can say for sure is that Max and Clara's adventures are far from finished. I expect at this point to end with a three-book series for Max and Clara, which several shorts and novella's set in the same Dead Aware world. Is there a short story you would like to see in this world? Tell me about it! (If you have an idea I write, that story will be dedicated to you with the choice to be a character within it!)

Dead Aware: Vagrant Youth, is a novella set in the Dead Aware world featuring a group of street kids in Vancouver at the start of FIRE.

Also keep an eye out for *Three and Fish* in an upcoming anthology *Undead Worlds 3*, a short story about where Three ended up almost a decade after the FIRE virus first covered the globe. Insider tip, here may be a furry friend involved.

To keep up to date on all my new fun stuff you can join my newsletter (which also includes a free, horrific short story called For the Love of a Child) and also follow me on Facebook (Eleanor Merry Author) or Instagram (zombie_ele).

ABOUT THE AUTHOR

Eleanor Merry was born and raised in beautiful Vancouver, BC and still lives there with her tiny human and her fiancé. The offspring of a fairy queen and an undead warlord, she was brought up with an appetite for terror and beauty.

When she isn't writing, she is a voracious reader with eclectic tastes which tends to lean towards horror and the twisted, however is known to indulge in dirty romances on the side. Her influences include authors such as Brian Keene, Mark Tufo, Richard Laymon and Tillie Cole. In all genres, nothing is off limits and she looks forward to sharing more of her own twisted and strange thoughts with the world.

www.ingramcontent.com/pod-product-compliance
Lightning Source LLC
Chambersburg PA
CBHW021201130626
46554CB00005B/1920